Charming
DR. FORRESTER

JEMMA FROST

Charming Dr. Forrester

The Garden Girls, Volume 0.5

Jemma Frost

Published by The Arrowed Heart, 2021.

CHARMING DR. FORRESTER

First edition. April 20, 2021.

ISBN: 978-1-955138-01-7

Written by Jemma Frost.

The Garden Girls

Charming Dr. Forrester
All Rogues Lead to Ruin

JEMMA FROST

For my dad and veterans like him

Charming DR.FORRESTER

Chapter One

1868 Manchester, England

A SHIVER TRAVELED DOWN Dr. Robert Forrester's spine at the realization that he was truly alone.

Watching Harry's coffin lower into a muddy grave, Robert thought it fitting that the typical Manchester rain hadn't ceased for his best friend's funeral. Grey drizzle seeped into his wool overcoat, while a chill settled over him, as if the ghost of his dead friend lingered nearby. It wouldn't surprise him if Harry decided to haunt him. Honestly, it'd be par for the course.

"We, therefore, commit his body to the ground..." The pastor droned on, as Robert wondered how his life had gone downhill so fast. Only six months earlier, he'd been preparing to resign as an army physician and partner with Harry with their own private practice. Then his mother had died unexpectedly while he was still overseas, and now his best friend was gone, as well.

Clenching clammy fists, he focused dark eyes on the mounds of dirt being shoveled over the casket...on the drops of water sliding down his neck...counting until he reached one hundred and started over. The repetitive practice helped to calm his roiling emotions. *Seventy-two, seventy-three, seventy-*

four... The numbers rang through his head, a single thread as thin as a spider's web grounding him to the present moment.

Harry had taught him the coping tactic — the trick helping him deal with his sporadic fits of madness. Night terrors, heart palpitations, flashes of memories from the war. Fits that, if found out, would surely result in him being shipped off to an asylum. *I can control this; that won't happen.*

A sob sounded to his left, overshadowing the pastor's calm, monotone voice. Harry's parents stood huddled together under an umbrella. His mother, a kindly woman with silver hair, held a handkerchief to her nose as tears trailed down her face, her shoulders shaking with spasms of grief. Mr. Rosing kept a stoic countenance, though the trembling at his mouth denoted a certain restrained emotion.

Robert regretted that this would be the last moment they had with their son as he remembered their happy send-off a week prior, when Harry and he had left for Manchester.

But only a few days later, Harry was struck by a runaway carriage. The shock of his sudden death had sent Robert into a spiral, wondering if he could've saved Harry if he'd been present. If he could've pulled him to safety or used his skills to revive him. A steady loop of scenarios tortured him as he sank deeper into despair and trying to drink the pain away only led to a terrible headache the next morning. Trying to reconcile his feelings of powerlessness left him drained; something that didn't help his already ragged state of mind.

After all, there would be no rescuing Harry.

Robert blinked away a blur of tears as his throat thickened, making it difficult to swallow. They'd formed a bond as close as brothers during the Crimean War. For twelve years, they'd worked together; two doctors providing medical attention to their assigned regiment.

Reaching one hundred in his mind, Robert decided there was nothing more for him to do. It was time he took his leave of this dreary weather — if only it was so easy to leave the grief behind.

Straightening, he approached the Rosings and offered his hand, "My condolences; Harry was a fine man; I know we'll all miss him."

Mrs. Rosing pulled his hand to her chest with a tight squeeze, "Oh, Robert, we're thankful he had your friendship to rely upon. I slept easier knowing he had you at his back all these years — especially during the war. To think, our Harry survived on the battlefield only to be taken from us now." Her voice cracked on the last word as her husband pulled her closer. Fearing his own breaking composure, he bade them farewell.

As he descended the hill where the small cemetery lay, his mind raced to figure out what to do with his career, his life. Without Harry's support, he couldn't afford to finance his own practice. Nor did he have any other ties to this town.

Not for the first time, he selfishly lamented the early death of his father.

Dr. Laurence Forrester came from three generations of physicians in Kettle Cross. A small village just south of the Scottish border, it had kept his father busy with the usual births and ailing elderly. The sleepy hamlet had suited Robert fine as he grew up, imagining one day taking over his father's practice and marrying a sweet village girl who would help him as his mother assisted his father.

Unfortunately, that dream came to an end after the senior Dr. Forrester suffered a stroke when Robert was fifteen. Too young to continue the family tradition, a new doctor was brought in to care for the village people, and he was left with no choice but to become a military doctor when he came of age: the only viable option for someone with his lack of funds and connections.

It turned out to be a timely occurrence, though, since Britain decided to go to war the same year he'd graduated from the Royal College of Surgeons in London. Joining became the patriotic and practical thing to do, and Robert didn't regret his decision, despite the issues it created within him.

While he reminisced, glows of light fought through the rain to reveal the front of the St. James Hotel. Only a few years old, the brick building boasted five stories of luxurious suites and first-class amenities. The owner, Mr. William Porter, previously from London, had decided to expand to Manchester, bringing the capital city's glamour to the industrial town.

Taking the marble steps leading to the front entrance two at a time, he ducked his head in a brief acknowledgement of the doorman before hustling to his suite upstairs. Plush carpet lined the hallways as sconces lit the way, the smell of fresh construction still hanging in the air.

Within the walls of his private rooms, he removed his coat and hat before stripping down to his trousers. He needed more than counting to calm his roiling emotions. Free of constricting clothing, he placed bare feet against the floor as he lay down and began doing sit-ups — the repetitive movement easing his mind.

Time passed slowly, the lone testament to the waning hour, a nub of a candle he'd lit upon entry. Laying flat, staring up at the ceiling, salty sweat burned his eyes as it dripped down his face. *Better than tears*, he thought.

A pleasant buzz settled over him as his heavy breaths filled the room. For a moment, his grief became shrouded by a numbing fog that kept the pain at bay. Closing his eyes, Robert drifted to a happier time, imagining his childhood home: the comforting smells of baking bread mingling with the stench of wet dog. He always came back to this day when Max, his dog, had saved him after he'd fallen into the lake. Not knowing how to swim yet, he'd panicked when the brackish water covered his head. Max had jumped in after him and pulled him to safety.

Once on solid ground, he'd run back home to his mother, crying on her shoulder about the terrifying incident. He remembered her comforting arms wrapping around him, squeezing him as his cries settled into hiccups and her warmth sank into his cold skin, the familiar scent of his mother surrounding him. This memory kept him sane — through the war and in the years since, whenever his thoughts threatened to overwhelm him. Which he feared would happen more frequently, now that he no longer had his mother and Harry. They'd always kept him grounded with a surplus of understanding and love. How would he cope now without their support?

Shaking his head, Robert sat up, determined to put aside such maudlin thoughts. They wouldn't want him dwelling in such a sad state. Ringing for a late dinner, he tried again to decide his next move, what path to take. To leave Manchester? Return to the military, to a post on the Continent?

He still had the funds intended to open the private practice, but it wouldn't be enough without Harry's share. Recalling his scheduled visit to see an old army acquaintance, Dr. Lane, he wondered if the man might be able to aid him in his decision. *If you can hold yourself together until then, and learn to control these episodes.*

Scrubbing a hand down his face, he prayed for a peace he doubted would ever come — after all, what did he have left in this world?

Chapter Two

Mrs. Johanna Milton perused the moisturizing creams on display in the hotel shop before she visited her best friend, Mrs. Ava Jensen. Recently out of mourning for her husband, she reveled in her newfound freedom. She'd been invited to Manchester for the summer, providing an excuse to escape the sedate countryside where she'd been sequestered.

Various scents washed over her as she sniffed each pot searching for the perfect gift. Lifting a cream labeled with orange blossom, she wrinkled her freckled nose at the tart affront to her senses. No, Ava definitely wasn't a citrus type of woman. Her friend exuded a calm demeanor perfect for making anyone feel at ease — unlike Johanna, whose fiery hair reflected her outgoing personality. But that quiet reserve had drawn Johanna to her when they were at Mrs. Hatter's School for Girls, and somehow, they'd balanced each other out.

She recalled one of the first balls they'd attended at school. They'd been sixteen and full of excitement, gowned in elaborate silk dresses with their hair done in the latest style. She'd been sure they'd be sought after.

However, Ava had retreated to a corner almost immediately. Reserved and uncomfortable in a crush of people, she'd hidden like a mouse, avoiding the potential social traps such an event held. But Johanna refused to let her friend become a wall-flower.

"You mustn't hide, Ava. Look at all the eligible men here! Who knows what the night may bring?"

Smiling at the memory, she remembered how she'd dragged Ava behind her and included her in every conversation. One that would even introduce Ava to her future husband. Though, they hadn't known at the time that a courtship would come a few short years later.

Johanna sighed as thoughts of those long-gone days caused a wisp of sadness to cloud her features. How she missed such simpler times — before their marriages and children and the subsequent death of her husband.

Though she'd wished for a love match during her Seasons out, her propensity for chatter drove away most potential suitors. That's when her uncle approached her father with his friend, Sir Howard Milton, who still needed an heir for his estate. Thus, the marriage contracts were drawn up, and she'd been married within a month of her twentieth birthday to a man nearing sixty.

While not enthusiastic about marrying a man so much older than her, she'd resigned herself to being a good wife. As time wore on without an heir, however, that hope withered like autumn leaves.

Useless! Unable to do the one damn thing I paid for you to do!

Johanna breathed in the soothing scent of lavender to calm her nerves at the memory when her courses had come once again. She blinked a few times as unexpected tears clouded her vision. Two years since his death, yet his words still had the power to cut her down.

Afraid of causing a scene, she quickly chose the familiar scent of rose, completed the purchase, and made her escape. The marble floor of the grand lobby shone as the crystal chandelier sparkled above. It was clear the owner hadn't spared any expense when it came to building such a venue. Frankly, she'd been impressed by the lavish accommodations, a surprise from the notoriously industrious Manchester.

Walking through the crowd of guests huddled around the front desk, she emerged onto the street where a line of hackneys waited for passengers. Their gleaming black tops reflected the weak sunlight as the horses stamped their hooves, eager to move.

"13 Helmstead Square, please," she said to the driver before settling in her seat, and they made their way through town.

It was similar to London, with its close buildings and the buzz of activity like a beehive. Since her marriage, she'd primarily resided at their country estate in Derbyshire, a far cry from the pace of things here. As she took in the passing scenery, a surprising bolt of energy shot through her; despite the smoke-filled air and downcast weather, she missed this life more than she'd thought.

Derbyshire provided a safe yet dull home, especially during her mourning when she hadn't been allowed to attend the few social events the country provided. And now she had to contend with Howard's younger brother, Richard, the heir since she was unable to provide a son. While pleasant enough to be around, she felt out of place as his sister-in-law when his children were of a similar age to her and visited with their families often.

Staring out the window, Johanna watched a woman with children in tow walking on the sidewalk, and her stomach tightened in yearning. Sitting back against the velvet seating, she placed a calming hand over the knot and fixed her eyes straight ahead. *One day*...Johanna prayed as she returned her attention to her current problem.

Perhaps she would talk to Ava about leaving Derbyshire. It held nothing for her now, despite the decade she'd spent there, and she was loath to return to London and her father's house. A shudder of denial shook her as she imagined having to deal with her father's gambling habit and her mother's criticisms.

Studying the stacks of smoke rising in the sky, Johanna had never felt an urge to move to an industrial city like Manchester with its scores of cotton mills, but perhaps it would be just what she needed. It might be best to make a fresh start, where her only acquaintance was her closest friend, and avoid the microscope of London society.

Seeing Ava's home approaching, she moved to the edge of her seat. Warming to the notion, she was eager to hear her friend's advice. Johanna knew she tended to move quickly and without thinking once she got an idea into her head. And uprooting her life warranted contemplation. Which is why she needed Ava's practical input.

As they came to a stop in front of the Georgian-style home and she alighted to the gravel drive, Johanna wondered what these next few months would hold while a renewed sense of hope filled her.

"JO, YOU MADE IT!" AVA hurried across the foyer to envelop her in a tight hug. Excited cries of "Aunt Jo, Aunt Jo!" bombarded her as she felt little hands clutch her skirts.

Laughing, Johanna extricated herself from her friend and her children's embrace, "Yes, yes, I'm here! What shall we do first?"

Multiple suggestions pelted her as the kids yelled out activities. Meeting Ava's eyes, a wordless agreement passed between them to talk later as they were dragged to the kids' playroom. The afternoon flew by in a blur of hide and seek then marbles before settling down for a book reading. At times, Johanna felt a pang in her heart as she imagined performing such tasks with her own family. But she shook off the melancholia it brought; being an honorary aunt was fulfilling enough.

Two nannies arrived to usher the children away for naps, and they were left in quiet as a tea cart was brought into the sitting room. Ava heaved a relieved sigh as she flounced down to the settee, worn out from their play.

"Sometimes I wonder what we were thinking having four children."

"I don't believe there was much *thinking* going on at all," Johanna commented, shooting a knowing look at her friend as she passed her a cup of hot tea.

"You make a good point," Ava said as an embarrassed blush spread over her cheeks. Johanna smiled. Ava and her husband, Mr. Grant Jensen, were one of the few love matches created during their Seasons out. The moment he'd met her reserved friend, he'd been smitten, trying his best to bring her out of her shell and eventually succeeding. Their courtship had been entertaining to watch — and a welcome distraction from her lack of such a relationship.

"How are your accommodations? Are you sure you don't want to stay with us? It wouldn't be an inconvenience," Ava asked again. Fussing with her skirt, Johanna considered the question.

It was difficult for Ava to understand why she'd prefer a hotel over the comforts of a family home with friends. But how could she explain that the children she loved as nieces and nephews were the very reason she couldn't stay? That seeing the shared look of adoration between her and Grant would be too painful?

Ava knew how much Johanna craved a family, but she assumed Johanna would eventually remarry?ever the pragmatic one of the pair?since Johanna was only three and thirty.

"It's more agreeable than I expected," she answered. "And I appreciate the offer; you know I love your family. But I don't want to intrude. St. James suits me fine...Speaking of living arrangements, I wanted to discuss the possibility of my leaving Derbyshire to settle here, perhaps? I miss the pace of city life and want to be closer to you and the children."

Ava's brows rose as she put her cup down. Sunlight sparkled on the painted flowers patterned across the porcelain, reminding Johanna of a tea set she'd received as a wedding gift. Now, it lay packed away in a storage room gathering dust?much like her.

"I didn't realize you wanted to leave...It's been your home for how many years now? Almost thirteen years? That's a lot of memories."

Johanna nodded, "Yes, though, not all good." She set down her own teacup as a determined glint entered her brown eyes. "I'm not ready to wilt away in the country. It might be nice to enter into Society again, and Manchester wouldn't be as intimidating as London. Besides, Richard's wife has taken over the care of the house. It's more their home than mine."

Which was true. Despite her long stay, it had always felt like a waystation for her?never meant to become a permanent fixture in her life, the hope of finding a true home always lingering in the back of her mind. Which had been impossible as long as she and Howard were married, but he was gone now, and maybe there was hope for her yet.

"Well, we'd enjoy having you here! The children would be thrilled to have their Aunt Jo so close. And I think it's about time you rejoined society...It's not too late for you to fall in love and have a family of your own."

Johanna ducked her head at the statement; she feared never finding either of those things. Yet wasn't that part of the reason for her impulsive decision to start over somewhere new? Along with another budding idea she'd kept tamped down but had grown in strength the longer she'd rusticated in the country. Ignoring Ava's comment, she said, "I was hoping to get more involved with the community. Find something more to do than attend parties. I've felt so restless; I need a project."

"Finding a husband is a worthy project," Ava pushed, tilting her head knowingly.

"As true as that may be, that's not what I have in mind," Johanna said. She knew it was unusual for a single woman to want something more than a husband, but she'd been married for eleven years, and it hadn't taken away her longing for more. If anything, it intensified the feeling.

After being seen as useless or frivolous for so long, she wanted to have a purpose. And she doubted having a loving spouse instead of a neglectful one would change such a need. Besides, another marriage wasn't guaranteed, at least she could control this part of her life.

Shrugging, Ava relented and suggested joining one of her women's organizations. "We spend a lot of time planning fundraisers and events, but it can be overwhelming when you're also trying to balance a family at home. Your help would be exactly what we need."

While Johanna wasn't opposed to such a thing, she'd hoped for a more substantial way of making a difference rather than doing what she'd always done: throwing parties and socializing with guests. It felt so hollow now, despite the funds that would be raised.

No, she wanted to be personally involved with those she helped; the problem was figuring out how a woman of her station interacted with those in need. It wasn't a proper thing to do. While Society put on a good show of helping the poor and under-served, they would never actually venture into those neighborhoods and speak with such people.

"I'll keep that in mind," she conceded before they moved on to other topics until it was time for her to leave. Hugging Ava good-bye, she waited for the hackney to arrive before directing the driver back to the hotel. The short drive passed quickly as she contemplated their conversation.

Sighing at the impossible task of figuring out her life, she stepped out of the cab and entered the palatial lobby. Covered in tasteful paintings and held aloft by towering columns, the space reminded her more of a Greek emperor's home than a hotel. As she began making her way to her room, an older woman addressed her.

"Pardon me, miss, but I adore your hat," she said, waving a hand towards her head, drawing attention to the beads of sweat that dotted her forehead.

Johanna had a brief thought of the poor woman overheating, but the pleasure of her compliment replaced any worry she might have felt. She enjoyed shopping and loved discussing her favorite pieces and where other women could find them. "Thank you! A Madame Mercier made it for me in London; she comes up with lovely creations."

She touched the green velvet hat with groups of silk flowers overflowing on one side. It toed the line between classy and ostentatious, which she was always careful to stay within. With such a boisterous personality at times, she tried to keep her clothing choices a bit more sedated — but only by a smidge. And now that she was beyond the black and greys of mourning, she felt even more bold in her fashion.

"You must?" the old woman's words were cut off as a strange look passed over her face before she tumbled to the ground.

"Oh!" Johanna rushed to catch the woman but only managed to rescue her head from hitting the marble floor. Shock tore through her as she cradled the unconscious woman's head, searching for any kind of injury. Glancing around at a few onlookers, one rational thought pushed to the forefront.

"Someone fetch a doctor! We need help!"

Chapter Three

Robert drew a hand through his hair, releasing a relieved sigh as he entered St. James. He imagined the hot bath waiting for him upstairs and the hearty meal afterward — eager for whatever the hotel's chef had on the menu tonight.

The day had been exhausting after helping a young couple who'd lost a stillborn babe. The woman's cries still rang in his ears as he attempted to shake off the feeling of helplessness pervading him.

No matter how hard he tried, he couldn't prevent every death, but that didn't mean each one didn't affect him?the weight bearing down, threatening to drown him one of these days. He should be grateful Dr. Lane had offered to let Robert see some patients to keep his skills sharp while he worked on his next steps. He considered approaching Lane with a proposal to buy into the practice and become partners, but every time he neared broaching the topic, a part of him remembered that it was Harry he was supposed to partner with, and a sense of betrayal washed over him.

An uproar rose to his left as his foot touched the first step of the staircase. Ignoring the noise, uncaring of what was happening, he'd started his ascent when someone called, "We need a doctor! Fetch a doctor!"

His hand clenched on the railing as he closed his eyes in resignation, a brief thought of letting someone else handle the problem raced through his head. There and gone as fast as a freight train. *I guess dinner will have to wait.*

Turning around, he moved towards the gathered crowd, pushing his way to the center where an older woman lay on the ground while a younger one held the woman's head in her lap. Her hat sat askew, mussing the gleaming red curls beneath. He heard her reassure the lady, "You'll be alright; don't you worry, we've called for a doctor."

Her soothing voice lapped at his body like the soft ripples of a pond — a strange reaction that he pushed aside. Springing to action, he knelt by the prone woman's side. "I'm Dr. Robert Forrester, ma'am. Can you tell me what happened?"

He set his bag down as he pulled out a stethoscope and listened to her heart and breathing as the younger woman answered, "One moment she stood talking to me, asking about my hat, then the next thing I knew she made a short little gasp and fell over. I tried to catch her as best I could."

He eyed the woman's frame compared to the larger woman at their feet, no doubt it had been a difficult feat to accomplish. "Do you know her name?" he asked after finding nothing to alarm him about her lungs and moving on to examine her limbs, checking for any injuries from a fall.

"No, we didn't have much time to acquaint ourselves before she fainted. I apologize for not knowing much more." Her gloved hands brushed over the woman's brow, a concerned frown wrinkling her forehead. Placing the stethoscope back in his bag, he retrieved a bottle of smelling salts and waved them under the older woman's nose. Her eyes popped open, shooting around wildly, trying to regain her bearings.

Leaning closer, he met her gaze, "It's all right, ma'am. I believe you just had an attack of the vapors. Does this happen often?" He knew some older women suffered these sorts of attacks when they allowed their corset strings to be tied too tightly, insisting on sticking to old trends despite the current advice against tight lacing.

"Yes, but I take a powder prescribed by the apothecary to keep them at bay. I'll confer with him about increasing the dosage." *That won't fix your problem.*

She sat up with the help of the woman behind her. Her obvious agitation at being surrounded by a dozen onlookers became apparent as she fidgeted with her hair and gloves, making sure she remained acceptably outfitted.

A booming voice sliced through the crowd as a man arrived with a team of footmen behind him, who began dispersing the gathered guests. "Everything's fine folks. Please carry on with your evening and leave the doctor to do his work." Upon closer proximity, he continued in a lowered voice, "Can I get you anything, Mrs. Wyland? I'm the owner, William Porter, and on behalf of the hotel, we pride ourselves in taking care of our guests, especially ones as beautiful as you."

His flirtatious comment brought a bright blush to the older woman's wrinkled face. Robert raised his eyes heavenward and scoffed at the obvious ploy to avoid any potential repercussions for the hotel at her accident. He could've warned Porter her incident was nothing but her damn fault — vanity being the main culprit. Now that the crisis was averted, his earlier fatigue returned along with irritation at being kept from his dinner over such a silly reason.

"No, thank you, sir, though your offer is much appreciated." Mrs. Wyland held the young woman's hand as she pulled herself to a standing position, swaying at the exertion. A wrinkled hand went to her stomach to steady herself.

"May I recommend asking your maid to have a lighter touch when tightening your corset? I believe that would drastically reduce your fainting problem," he mentioned, restraining his annoyance. The woman in question huffed in effrontery while the redhead stepped forward.

"Excuse me, sir, but that is most inappropriate of you. A gentleman doesn't comment on a lady's underthings." Her shoulders pushed back as she straightened to scold him, sparks shooting from her brown eyes.

"*Excuse me*, miss," he repeated, a sarcastic note entering his tone, "As I'm the medical professional, you'll understand if I don't take your advice on how I should conduct myself with a patient. Especially one who's decided to ignore prevailing medical advice, choosing to cling to a style twenty years out-of-date."

Her eyes widened at his rude remark, her pretty mouth dropping to expel a rough breath. "How dare you..."

Porter cut her off, raising his hands in a gesture of peace, "Ladies, I apologize for my friend, Dr. Forrester. He's had a long day; he can't be held responsible for such behavior at the moment." Turning to Robert, he motioned towards the stairs, a beseeching look in his eyes, "Why don't you go up to your room for a hot meal; I'm sure that will set you back to rights."

Accepting the reprieve, Robert started to leave when Porter placed a hand on his shoulder, "Oh, I almost forgot, if you're free tomorrow, I'd like to see you in my office for a quick meeting."

Wondering if he could be evicted for insulting guests, Robert nodded before dipping into a semblance of a bow and making his escape. His lips tightened in a grimace. It looked like tomorrow would be another red letter day.

AFTER THE RUDE DOCTOR left, Mr. Porter apologized again for his unacceptable behavior. "He's overworked, you see; he spends his days offering healthcare in the rookeries. You can imagine the daily tragedies he deals with ."

Johanna softened a little at the information, her body losing some of its rigidity, and refocused on Mrs. Wyland and Mr. Porter. The charming hotel owner placed a warm hand on both Johanna and Mrs. Wyland as he addressed them. "Are you sure there's nothing I can do to make up for your terrible incident? Perhaps one of Chef Le Beau's special desserts? They've been known to perk up a lady's spirits." A handsome grin encouraged them to accept his offer.

"Thank you, young man. I think that might be just the thing I need; it might calm my nerves," Mrs. Wyland agreed wearily, her fall starting to take its toll. "Could you have it sent to my rooms? I might lie down for a spell."

"Of course, madam. I'll see to it at once. And you, Mrs. Milton?" After her negative response, he bowed before leaving them to fetch Mrs. Wyland's dessert. The lobby still bustled with activity as if nothing had happened, leaving Johanna feeling a bit useless now and unsure of what to do. Wringing her hands, she bit her lip. It wasn't like she knew Mrs. Wyland, but how to extricate herself from such an unusual situation? It wasn't every day that she caught a swooning woman.

Thankfully, the woman in question spoke first. "My dear girl, I don't know what I would've done without you here; you were a godsend in my time of need."

Blushing at the high praise, she tried to defer, "Nonsense; anyone would have done the same thing. I'm just glad you're alright."

"No, you have a way about you. Even during my unconscious state, I heard your calming words of encouragement like an angel sent from above. Or like my old Aunt Agnes who spoke to me once at a seance I attended at Lady Canne's."

Johanna's eyebrows rose in surprise at the turn their conversation had taken. She knew seances were all the rage these days, but she wasn't sure she believed in spirits talking from the grave. And while Johanna had been trying to comfort the woman, she'd mostly filled the silence with nervous chatter as was her habit. But now she wondered if maybe this wasn't a sign of something more for her particular abilities. Could she somehow turn what she viewed as a useless skill into some helpful asset? But how?

As if answering her unspoken question, Mrs. Wyland continued, "You know, that gruff doctor could use something of your manner; his is altogether unpleasant."

A speculative gleam lit her face as she followed the line of stairs to the next floor where the doctor had disappeared. Perhaps Mrs. Wyland had a point. Of course, she knew nothing of medicine and the man didn't seem particularly friendly. But

Mr. Porter *had* said the man was overworked. Maybe it had been a particularly grueling day; she'd had a few of those herself where she'd acted out of character. Besides, despite his delivery, he'd made a valid point about the tightlacing.

It couldn't hurt to test the waters, to see where this path may lead.

Resolved to try her luck with Dr. Forrester, Johanna clasped the older woman's gloved hand in farewell. "Please send for me if you require anything and try to rest tonight!" Mrs. Wyland nodded, and they went their separate ways.

As Johanna went upstairs to her suite, a long-forgotten memory resurfaced of when she'd comforted a maid, Lucy, whose son had died of a fever. Johanna had found the woman crying over a table she'd been dusting, hunched over as her tears wet the polished wood. Although Lucy had been afraid of losing her job due to such a display, Johanna had reassured her before placing an arm over her trembling shoulders. They only stood like that for a few minutes, but afterward Lucy had expressed her gratitude for Johanna's presence. And she had to admit that it felt good to help.

Her mind opened with all sorts of possibilities, Johanna spent the remainder of the evening trying to channel Ava's practical nature and come morning, she had a plan to approach the impertinent doctor.

Chapter Four

"**I**'ll cut to the chase: I've heard rumors that you won't be moving forward with your plans to open a private practice."

Robert sat in front of Porter's mahogany desk, his hands resting on the soft leather arms of his chair. Thick tomes covered one wall as a fireplace lay dormant on his right. He studied the spacious room and wondered if he'd ever have such a place to work. *Not bloody likely*. One didn't become a physician for the pay.

"You've heard correctly," Robert said. He didn't know how the news had traveled so quickly, but he supposed that was the way of gossip.

The early hour reflected through the windows, soft sunlight attempting to lend a cheery air to the masculine atmosphere. He hadn't been sure Porter would be available so early considering men of his stature didn't start their business day until ten in the morning, but when he'd arrived at Porter's office before heading to the rookery, his secretary had shown him inside.

"Excellent!" Porter paused as he realized the callous way that sounded. "I mean to say: I'm sorry for the loss of your friend. Dr. Rosing seemed like a fine fellow. However, without his support, that leaves you a bit in the wind, doesn't it? Which means you might be open to my proposal."

A furrow formed between Robert's brows. What sort of proposal would a wealthy hotelier have for a former army surgeon? Shoulders tensing in preparation for whatever scheme he was about to hear, he knew he'd regret counting his blessings too quickly after Porter made no mention of the previous night's debacle. An image of the spirited, young woman appeared before floating away like a puff of smoke. *She doesn't concern you.*

Resting an arm on a bookshelf, Porter swept a finger over the dark wood before saying, "It came to me last night after your assistance with Mrs. Wyland. As a man in the hospitality business, I want to serve all my guests' potential needs. And it occurred to me that having an on-site physician would be beneficial to patrons and my employees." Turning towards Robert, Porter continued, "I'd like to offer you the position. Your room and board would be taken care of as you stay here, and I will compensate you fairly for your time. You'll have two free days a week to do with as you please, perhaps staying on to help your friend, Dr. Lane. What do you say?"

Robert calculated the pros and cons of such a position. On one hand, he'd live rent free in a more opulent home than he would've in a flat of his own. And the ailments shouldn't be too terrible at such a high-scale residence. But he'd be living where he worked. Never truly able to leave work behind. Though what did that matter, he inwardly scoffed. It's not like he had anything better going on in his life. No wife or family to speak of.

In fact, he was going nowhere fast as he'd failed to come up with viable job options in the days since Harry's funeral. If Porter wanted to hire a full-time, live-in doctor, who was he to look a gift horse in the mouth?

Rising to his feet, decision made, Robert reached out to shake Porter's hand, "I'm in."

AFTER GIVING PORTER a list of supplies he'd need for his medical office, Robert spent the next few days helping Dr. Lane as he waited for the proper preparations to be made at the hotel. Porter had even upgraded him to a suite upon his employment, which Robert appreciated. On the fourth day, he was summoned to the lobby and escorted by a bellhop named Henry to a room towards the back of the building where Porter stood with a ring of keys spinning idly in his hand.

The waxed pine door had two glazed glass panes where a nameplate reading, "Dr. Robert Forrester, Hotel Physician", stood proud. A burst of pride and something akin to excitement bubbled within Robert at the sight. On the Crimean Peninsula, in the midst of war, there was hardly a place for a plaque of his own. A temporary tent pitched in a field didn't warrant the dignity of proprietorship.

"Ah, Dr. Forrester, there you are! Thank you, Henry, that will be all for now," Porter said as he waved the boy off. The boy dipped his head, blonde curls falling over his eyes, before scurrying back to the main lobby.

Porter placed the key into the door's lock and asked, "Ready?"

Without waiting for a response, he swung the door open to reveal a large room that could be partitioned into two with a large curtain that hung gathered on one wall. Gleaming metal instruments reflected the bright gas lights lining the walls, while a raised examination bed looked out on the alley behind the hotel.

Astonishment rang through Robert at the sight. He spied a sphygmograph and wondered how Porter had gotten his hands on so much, so quickly. "I suppose you had this lying around..." He placed a hand on a tank labelled "nitrous oxide". "How the devil did you get this set up so quickly?"

"Money can buy anything; no matter how short the notice." Porter shrugged as if this fact had always been true in his life. Which caused a pang of jealousy before he tamped it down with a helping of gratefulness. For Robert, who'd grown up without a silver spoon, then forced to make do with run-down military equipment, this was more than he'd ever expected. Even if Harry had been alive, they'd planned on getting by with used equipment until they could afford to buy newer items.

"I see...Well, I thank you, and more importantly, so will your guests and employees," Robert said. "Speaking of which, I was thinking it might be beneficial to do a standard exam for the hotel staff. To get to know everyone and make everyone comfortable."

"I'll have my assistant send out a notice to the staff. If there's anything else you need or supplies begin to run low, let me know." Checking the watch pinned to his vest, he let it drop back down before saying, "I have another appointment, but now that we have everything settled, I think we should celebrate tonight at my club. To christen our new partnership."

"I'm not sure that would be appropriate considering you're my employer." Robert's eyebrows rose in surprise at the offer. Although Porter was about his age, they occupied vastly different social circles.

Porter waved a dismissive hand. "Nonsense! We can work together and be friends. You're an educated man and, frankly, could use a friend considering what happened to poor Dr. Rosing. No, we shall meet tonight, and you can regale me with stories of your time abroad."

"How did you know...?"

"I always make it my business to know my employees, Forrester. Your report mentioned a time in the Crimean War during your military stint."

Robert felt like he'd been hit by a stray cannonball. His chest ached with a sudden pressure as his heart rate ticked upward. The mention of Harry and the war threw him off-kilter; he hadn't expected Porter to dive into his past.

"Yes, Harry and I served together. However, I still don't think it would be wise. What would the rest of your employees think of me getting preferential treatment?"

"I don't give a damn what anyone thinks; I own the establishment and I can associate with whomever I want. Meet me in the lobby at nine tonight; I'm not taking no for an answer." And with that decree, Porter swept out of the room like the whirlwind he resembled.

Releasing a heavy breath, Robert walked around the office and let the familiar medical instruments calm him as he tried to decide the best course of action. Perhaps one night out wouldn't be so bad, he reasoned. It would satisfy Porter and probably deter him from this friendship pursuit.

A wry grin tugged at his lips. Most employers wouldn't lower themselves to associating with the help, yet Robert had managed to find the one man in the whole of England who would. Essentially, ordering him to socialize outside of work.

Harry must be having a good laugh wherever he was. Putting that night's activities out of his mind, Robert let the thrill of his new job run through him. Porter's request aside, it looked like things might finally be looking up for him.

Chapter Five

Johanna woke up early to be downstairs in time to intercept Dr. Forrester. She wasn't sure of his schedule, but at the moment, catching him on his way to work seemed like the best option. *A fat lot of good that's done me.*

It'd almost been a week, and she still hadn't seen him. Frustrated, she'd spent each night imagining ways to broach the topic of helping him until exhaustion forced her to sleep. The lack of rest was beginning to show in the purple shadows under her eyes, but she knew she may only have one chance to pitch her idea, and it had to be flawless.

Donning her most serviceable dress, a light gray satin with understated trimmings, she felt as close to the role of doctor's assistant as she could muster. Her usual brightly colored outfits, she instinctively knew, would not go over well with the austere doctor. No, best to stick with a plain, no-nonsense outfit when she approached him.

Checking her appearance one more time in the hallway mirror, Johanna smiled to boost her confidence then hurried downstairs. The empty lobby felt like a different world compared to the usual crowd of people it held; activities the night before kept most of its guests abed which worked out perfectly for her.

She preferred not to have an audience when she spoke with Dr. Forrester. A woman conversing with a single man alone would certainly be cause for gossip, not that anyone knew her here. A frown wrinkled her brow as she realized, she had no idea if he was unattached or not. He could have a whole family upstairs! Shaking her head at the wayward thought, she tried to focus on the task ahead of her.

"Good day, sir! No, no...Dr. Forrester, what a coincidence! No..." Johanna muttered under her breath. Each practiced opening seemed out of place as she paced across the black and white checkered floor. It put her in mind of a chess game, and she was the lowly pawn trying to decipher the moves that would land her a checkmate.

Taking a stance to the side of the staircase, she bounced on the balls of her feet in anticipation and nerves. The lone concierge stared at her in confusion before moving on with his tasks. Dismissing how peculiar she must look and watching the steps like a hawk, she went over her list of talking points to convince Dr. Forrester of her assets.

Admittedly, the list was short. She had the gift of gab and, according to Mrs. Wyland, a soothing presence. Was this enough to grant her request? Wringing her gloved hands, it occurred to her that perhaps she should've spoken with Ava instead of spending the past few days focused on how to win over Dr. Forrester.

Maybe she was being too hasty committing to this decision, rushing headlong into a disaster. It had seemed like the perfect solution when Mrs. Wyland suggested it; now she wasn't so sure.

As if her insecurities had beckoned him, daring her to forge ahead, Dr. Forrester descended the marble stairs at a hurried gait, his leather bag swinging by his side. His black hair was neatly styled and revealed hints of silver at his temples. Johanna recalled that he hadn't looked much older than her the night they'd met despite the deepened frown lines on his face. As he neared the bottom, he kept his head down, and only on the last step, when she moved into his pathway, did he look up, startled by her appearance.

"What the devil?" The rough question punctured a bit of her confidence; clearly, the past few days had done nothing to improve his attitude. *Why am I doing this again?*

Rallying, she pasted a broad smile on her face and said, "Dr. Forrester, I'm Mrs. Johanna Milton. You may not remember, but we met when?"

"I remember," he said, "You're married?" He cast a sidelong glance over her body, following the shine on her shoes up to her simple gray hat, before sidestepping to continue his trek out the door.

"Widowed, actually," she explained before trailing him across the lobby. He took one stride for every two of her rushed steps. The visual evoked the sense of an eager puppy chasing a bird across the yard. "I wanted to speak about accompanying you on your medical visits. I believe?"

"Absolutely not," he interrupted again, then stopped and turned, causing her to run into him. A pleasant waft of sandalwood tickled her nose as he steadied her with his hands on her arms. Gaze narrowing, he asked, "Why would you want to join me anyway? We're strangers."

She struggled to regain her composure as all her carefully planned out points flew out of her head. She found herself arrested by the dark color of his eyes, so much richer than her own plain brown, as she realized he was of a similar height to her own. Lungs struggling for breath, she couldn't tell if it was because of her rush to keep up with him or their close proximity. *Nonsense, pull yourself together.*

"That may be true, but Mrs. Wyland mentioned how it might be helpful for your patients to have a calm presence talking to them as you worked. Serving as a sort of distraction." She grasped at tendrils of her argument and remembered, "Oh, and Mr. Porter said that you were overworked! I could help lessen the burden."

"And how do you propose to do that? Unless you have a medical degree that I'm unaware of, you'd be adding to my so-called *burden* because, last time I checked, *talking* was not part of the curriculum at the Royal College." His dismissive words stung as he set her away from him and continued his journey outside. The morning light shone on his clean-shaven jaw as he left her behind.

"I understand your trepidation," she said, a frustrated huff flying out of her as she tried to keep up with him again. The street sidewalk provided little room for conversation as they dodged other pedestrians taking a morning stroll. "But I still believe I'd be a great benefit to you. Despite my background, don't you need an assistant? You can't possibly enjoy doing so much work alone."

She guessed at his feelings. Most men she knew had numerous people beneath them to handle the mundane, day-to-day details. Her late husband, Howard, for his part, had multiple assistants visiting to update him on the state of his property and investments. Granted, a city physician was a world away from a country squire, but work was work, no matter the profession, and people always needed help.

"My work is my own, and I appreciate not having someone underfoot. Now, run along, Mrs. Milton."

Her mouth tightened at his condescending tone; it was really beginning to annoy her. Tugging on his arm, the hard muscle bunching under her grip, she stopped him from going any further. Scrambling to stand in front of him, she placed her hands on her hips to show she was not to be trifled with, and to allow her to take in more air as her body tried to adjust to keeping up with his stride.

"Listen, sir, I would be an asset to you, *a veritable boon* for your patients who are surely so afraid of your harsh demeanor they cower like rabbits when a wolf nears." He opened his mouth again, but this time she raised a hand to stop him in his tracks. "I'm not finished yet. I'm calm during a crisis as you witnessed yourself with Mrs. Wyland, and I can provide a friendly distraction to patients as you work."

A pause fell between them as her heavy breaths filled the space while he maintained an irritatingly normal breathing pattern. The only sign of any reaction to her outburst was the clenching of his fist at his side and a slight twitch at the corner of his eye.

"I'm done now; you can speak," she said, eyebrows raising. Normally, she wasn't given to such displays of emotion and felt a frisson of remorse at being so forthright. But it grated on her nerves that he wouldn't even consider her proposal.

He took a deep breath while his jaw shifted as if mulling over which words to use to best skewer her on the spot—at least that's what she imagined. "While I appreciate your gracious concern for my patients..." Sarcasm dripped like venom, giving the distinct impression he felt the exact opposite of appreciation, "I, again, decline your offer. You have no medical experience, and though you may have a talented mouth..." He paused to stare at her lips causing a fierce and inappropriate blush to rise in her, "I'd stick to what you know best: talking about the latest fripperies and gossip and leaving actual patient care to me: an educated doctor with nearly thirteen years' experience."

His barb hit its mark, reminding her of Howard's insults. It almost made her give up, doubt creeping in, questioning if she really could help him. But while she couldn't deny his point, she knew she was worth more than being relegated to social parties speaking nonsense. *Try once more, and if he refuses, you'll know to move on.*

"You're right; I do know the best seamstresses and where to place an order for exotic perfumes. And, yes, I can tell you who was caught sneaking out of whose ball, and while you laugh, these skills have come in handy for most of my life. I'm not ashamed of them." No, shame may not be the correct definition for what she felt, but she wasn't proud of *only* being seen as a chatterbox.

Nevertheless, she forged ahead, "Now, I want to put them to better use. Don't you think your patients would appreciate someone providing comfort as you saw to their ills? Wouldn't it be worth exploring?" She implored him to give her a chance.

Surely, he could see the benefits of having a comforting presence around to ease someone's suffering.

Reaching out a beseeching hand, she squeezed his arm—an impulsive act she immediately regretted. It wasn't exactly proper behavior to touch a man so openly, let alone a stranger, even if she was intrigued by the hard muscle underneath. *Where did that come from?*

Removing her hand, she tried to rally, determined not to admit defeat.

ROBERT'S EYES DROPPED to where Mrs. Milton had touched him, the warmth sending a shot of pure adrenaline through him. He looked up into her hopeful, brown eyes, but he would not be swayed — no matter how attractive he found her.

He didn't need an uneducated woman assisting him. This wasn't like his mother helping his father, or even the wife he'd imagined taking had he stayed in Kettle Cross. Mrs. Milton was a lady accustomed to a different sort of life. Who knew what her reaction would be to seeing an open wound, or infected sores?

"The answer is no." He marched around her, hearing the tapping of her heels as she rushed to catch up to him. She would tire of this pace and give up — at least he prayed that would be the case. Her presence agitated him, made annoying thoughts of desire crop up when he thought he'd put those aside.

Years had passed since his last liaison with a woman, and it was what he preferred. Women conjured up romantic notions

of the military doctor needing their tender, loving care to become whole again. *No, thank you.* He was *whole* all by himself; besides, the occasional attacks he suffered from wouldn't
be cured by a woman.

"I'm not taking no for an answer, sir," she said, lifting her
skirts to avoid the muck as they neared Devil's Haven, one of
the rookeries north of the city center. The slim ankle revealed
should not have affected him, sturdy black boots covering most
of it, but he imagined the delicate joint and how sensitive it
would be under his mouth...*Enough!*

He gave a mental shake as he focused his attention forward; he didn't have time for this. Mrs. Jenkins was expecting
him to check on her gout, and he didn't need a pretty distraction like Mrs. Johanna Milton. He'd already put off the visit to
attend to his new duties at the hotel.

"And I'm not taking you any further." He stopped to order
her back to the hotel, "Turn around and go back to St. James.
You don't belong here."

With the dictate handed down, he crossed his arms over
his chest, waiting for her to follow the command. Mirroring
his stance, she faced him, rebellious waves radiating from her. It
would seem the adage about red-haired women and their tem-
pers wasn't completely unfounded.

They stood in a battle of wills for another minute before
her shoulders finally dropped, and she released a sigh of resignation. "I will leave you to your work, sir. However, I can't
guarantee I won't ask again at a later time."

He figured as much, but that would be trouble for another
day. Grinding his teeth, he pulled out his pocket watch and
noted the time. This entire exchange was making him late.

"That's your prerogative, but my answer will be the same. Now, I must go; you've already made me tardy for my patient."

With an abbreviated bow, he left her behind. *What was she thinking?* Offering her services to him. It was an odd request, no matter her altruistic reasoning. A gently-bred lady didn't bother with work; there was no need.

Winding through tight alleyways, he stepped over trash and sleeping homeless people. With prosperity came a larger disparity in wealth. These were the poor folks left behind; the ones who couldn't work at one of the many factories dotting Manchester. A contrast to the lady in question.

Here was need. But due to circumstances, these people couldn't find work. Yet, Mrs. Milton who, judging by her attire and comportment, didn't require money, wanted to join his practice. Her badgering made it seem like the matter was of vast importance to her. It didn't make sense.

Besides, he thought grimly, he had a hard enough time focusing with his grief over Harry still looming. Replacing him with Mrs. Milton seemed wrong and asking for trouble. With his nightmares becoming more frequent, no doubt due to his emotional turmoil, one more disturbance to his life may very well be the straw to break the camel's back.

Coming to Mrs. Jenkins's door, he pushed all thoughts of Mrs. Milton, Harry, and fatigue aside and knocked twice before entering the dark room. He needed to focus on what mattered, not some flame-haired woman.

Chapter Six

For the next few days, Johanna contemplated her next steps. Her initial meeting with Dr. Forrester had not gone as planned, and she admitted that she might have acted in haste. She hardly knew the man yet leapt at the possibility of aiding him all on Mrs. Wyland's recommendation—someone else who could barely be categorized as an acquaintance.

Sighing, she set the book she'd been reading down and gazed out the blurred window. The rain had been pouring down all morning with no sign of stopping. It was one of the few things she missed of Derbyshire: the smell of rain watering the countryside. Everything appeared so fresh and revitalized afterwards. Here it washed away the lingering scent of cotton and smoke, but the streets and buildings remained as dull as ever.

Johanna wondered again if it would be a mistake to move to Manchester, after all. But no matter the drab locale, the city still provided more opportunities than the sleepy village near Howard's estate. Unless she could think of a way to turn her particular talents into something useful for the small hamlet. Now that's something worth exploring...

It would save her from uprooting her life, the little she had in Derbyshire anyway. Rising from her seat to move to the writing desk, she pulled out a sheet of paper and a pen and listed possible ideas. Forget Dr. Forrester; she could assist the local physician, Dr. Lindon, with his patients. Or perhaps take on a supportive role with the milliner or dressmaker. She didn't need to be paid; it could be an advisory position as she was often asked about her own style. Of course, she'd never heard of such a thing, but that didn't mean it wouldn't be useful!

Excited, she began outlining her next steps when a knock at the door sounded. Glancing up, she wondered who would be calling but waited for Emma, her lady's maid, to answer.

After a few moments, Emma entered with a letter in hand. "This just arrived for you, ma'am."

"Thank you, Emma." Taking the folded sheet in hand, she recognized the seal of Marlow Gate. Strange...Why would her brother-in-law, Richard, be writing to her?

Breaking the red wax seal, she read the neatly-printed words as her heart sank into her stomach. While not said outright, he suggested that it would be best if she stayed in Manchester or returned to her parents' home in London. He thought she'd be happier with her own family. Richard said he would send her things to wherever she preferred. And of course, he'd provide a small stipend to keep her comfortable.

Johanna wiped a stray tear as she reached the end of the missive. The amount Richard had allotted for her upkeep would hardly cover another month's stay at the hotel. No, she'd be forced to find some boarding house if she wanted to stay off the streets.

While she'd never formed deep connections with Howard's family, she didn't think they cared so little for her to effectively throw her out without any true means of support. As Howard's widow, she assumed she'd always have a home there, despite

Richard moving in as the heir. It seemed her original plan of possibly moving to Manchester had become reality and a necessity.

She couldn't go back to London to live with her parents. Part of the reason why she'd been more amenable to marrying Howard was to escape them and create her own loving family, though she'd failed. If she moved back now, it would be a return to cold family dinners and her mother's constant barrage of comments about needing to remarry. *It'd be better than starving and freezing in an alleyway.*

We're not there yet, she told herself. She still had time to earn some extra funds before she had to resort to such drastic measures. Refolding the letter and setting it down, Johanna rubbed her temples where a headache was beginning to form. She truly was adrift now with no home and no purpose.

A salty tear fell to the manila paper creating a rapidly expanding circle. Another soon joined it as she let a wave of helplessness wash over her. Thirty-three years of age and what did she have to show for it? A dead husband and a penchant for talking. *Pathetic.*

Sniffling, she drew a handkerchief from her pocket and dabbed at her wet cheeks. Soon she would visit with Ava again and decide how to proceed. But for now, she would wallow in self-pity.

A KNOCK SOUNDED ON the door and Robert heard a quiet voice say, "Sir, this is Mr. John Flannery, my uncle. He's new to the hotel, and I thought he should see you."

The young bellhop he'd met previously showed an older man into Robert's office. He set aside the file he'd been working on and gestured to the raised bed in front of them.

"Come in, Mr. Flannery; you can take a seat there. Is something paining you?" he asked, pulling the stethoscope from around his neck, preparing to begin a preliminary exam.

"It's not that bad, doc. Young Henry's concerned for nothing," said the elder Flannery. He pulled his collar down to reveal what was troubling his nephew. Robert kept a straight face as he eyed the large red boil that stood out like a beacon on the man's neck.

"It doesn't look like nothing. May I?" After Flannery's consent, he leaned in and carefully felt around the lump. The man jumped at the contact. Lifting his hands, he retreated until his back met one of the counters lining the wall. "I apologize for the pain, but I fear Henry was right to bring you to me. This is infected and will need to be lanced."

Sighing, Flannery ran a rough hand down his grizzled cheek. "Well, I guess you should get to it then; I dealt with worse in the military, anyhow."

Robert froze at the mention of Flannery's service. "Military?"

"Yes, sir. I've just returned home from the Continent. Tired of sleeping in tents and the like. My sister's boy, here, managed to talk Mr. Porter into hiring me as one of the general handymen."

"I see." Pulling a cart of his supplies closer to Flannery, Robert dabbed a linen cloth with carbolic acid before cleaning the infected area. He noticed a trembling in his hands but commanded it to steady itself. "It's fortunate that Mr. Porter was able to assist you."

*One, two, three...*His breathing stuttered in his throat, never quite filling his lungs all the way. He worried the sound of his pounding heart would notify Flannery and Henry of his distress. *Not now...Dammit! Control yourself!*

"You're a military man, aren't you? Henry mentioned you moved here after completing your service." Robert cursed the gossiping employees and their nosy natures. One would think being in the hospitality business would instill a sense of keeping people's lives private.

"You've heard correctly." Robert said, refusing to elaborate, as he picked up a scalpel off the tray of instruments in front of him. The sharp metal reflected the light above. A reflection that shook as Robert willed his hand to still. Moving behind the man, he tilted Flannery's head to the right to create a clear field of work.

"Now, I'm going to make a slight cut to drain the infected fluid. Henry you might want to look away for this part." The young man's eyes widened, the color leaching from his face, before facing the wall.

"Alright, doc. Just get it over with."

Holding his breath, Robert placed the blade against the red bulge. He pressed lightly to create a small opening until his hand spasmed, forcing him to pause. *Take a moment; you're in control.* Once he'd calmed himself again, he proceeded with the cut. The old man hissed and tried to jerk away, but Robert followed, holding fresh gauze to catch the bleeding.

It's alright; you did it. Within minutes, the blood began clotting, and after wiping the area again with antiseptic, he wrapped a bandage around Flannery's neck. A list of instructions on how to care for the wound tumbled from him before he sent the older man on his way, Henry towing behind him.

Once they'd left, panic set in. Robert's frayed control unraveled as he locked the door and slid down to the gleaming floor. Dropping his head into his hands, he groaned at the peril his unreasonable reaction had put his patient in—not to mention his own career. If he hadn't been able to steady his hand, he could've killed the man...

This was the closest one of his attacks had gotten to overriding his control and endangering someone. Clearly, his coping strategies weren't working anymore, but he didn't know what to do. Short of quitting medicine, what were his options? And what could he do if he wasn't a doctor? It's not like he had reserves of money stashed away to support himself.

His eyes caught on three drops of blood marring the floor. The dark russet color filled his vision as he tried to remember what number he was on. *Eighty-one, eighty-two...Think of Max. Think of mother.*

Slowly, his mind calmed, and he no longer felt like his heart was about to leap from his chest, the vise-like hold on his lungs releasing. Inhaling through his nose then exhaling through his mouth, he waited a few more minutes before pulling himself up to remove the blood spots.

It was taking longer for his old techniques to be effective which didn't bode well for his future. It seemed he'd have to figure out a new way to beat his demons?if only he knew where to start.

Chapter Seven

Market Street buzzed with activity as Johanna made her way to Mrs. Langston's Millinery. After a good cry and visit with Ava, who'd tried her best to console her, they'd agreed that there was no reason she couldn't put her plan into action in Manchester rather than Derbyshire. Indeed, the city overflowed with shops where she could potentially land a position. Perhaps this was for the best!

"Pardon me," Johanna stepped aside as a woman in a striped walking dress left the store with her two daughters lagging behind. Once they'd passed, she left the crowded sidewalk to enter a quiet, shaded room that felt like a world away. Feathers and ribbons of all types fluttered in the window as fabrics lined one wall. Ladies milled about feeling the texture of one swatch before testing the weight of another.

Soon enough, a short woman with impeccable styling greeted her. "Good morning, madam. May I help you find something in particular?"

Pasting on a confident smile, Johanna said, "I'm actually looking for the proprietress. Would that be you?"

The woman nodded before lifting her arms to encompass the shop. "Yes, I'm Mrs. Langston. How may I help you?" She gestured for Johanna to move out of the main path of ladies entering the store. Following her lead, Johanna reminded herself of what she had to offer and launched into her spiel.

She noticed the slight widening of Mrs. Langston's eyes as she began but pushed through, hoping the woman would give her a chance to finish. "So, you see, I could be a great benefit to your store, and you'd be the most fashion-forward milliner in the city. No one else has a lady willing to espouse her expertise on styles in-store, helping to promote sales."

"My dear…" Mrs. Langston said. "I'm afraid that's because we consider ourselves to be that very expert. Women come to me for my unique creations for I know what best works for a client and have the skill to make it happen."

Deflating, Johanna forged on. A rush of nerves sent her head spinning, but she needed to remain calm to convince Mrs. Langston of her usefulness. "I understand, but to be frank, and I mean you no insult, I would be offering a different perspective. One from a peer, a confidant, since I run in the same social circles as your clientele."

"*Let me be frank*, Mrs. Milton is it? I have no need for an advisor, as you put it, and neither do my clients. To put it plainly, you are unnecessary. Now, if you'll excuse me." Mrs. Langston walked away without a backward glance and headed towards a gaggle of women by the teal peacock feathers.

Unnecessary.

Useless.

The words were a familiar refrain as the light feminine voice of Mrs. Langston dropped to the deeper tones of Howard. He relished every opportunity to remind her of her failings, especially when it came to conceiving his heir. She could've told him not to bother; she berated herself enough for the both of them when it came to that particular defect.

A ringing bell chimed as more patrons entered the shop and she noticed Mrs. Langston eyeing her. *Time to leave.* Hustling out the door, she glanced up and down the street, trying to decide which direction to go first as she placed a calming hand over her belly.

A pit the size of a walnut sat in her stomach.

And as the afternoon wore on, and she was turned away from shop after shop, that walnut grew to be a watermelon, sitting as heavy and ominous as the grey clouds above. Towards the end of her journey, she'd ventured into the more rundown part of town where, instead of being politely shown the door, she'd been eyed with suspicion. A lady working in trade? Something had to be wrong with her. And perhaps they were right.

But what choice did she have? If she didn't find employment soon, she'd be forced to leave St. James Hotel for cheaper accommodations, and she wasn't prepared to live in a boarding house with strangers. It'd be like living in a dormitory at school again, except less fun and possibly more dangerous. Who knew who she'd be living next to?

Feeling tears well up for the hundredth time that day, Johanna looked up at the sky and blinked them away. It'd be no use crying on the street. Thunder rumbled overhead, jolting her out of her melancholy; if she wasn't quick, she'd be soaked to the bone before she made it home.

A myriad of scenarios raced through her mind like the horses on Derby Day. Each possible outcome to her situation worse than the last and inching ahead of the others, eager to be the winner. As she finally made her way through the hotel lobby to her suite, she saw Dr. Forrester conversing with Mr. Porter. The two men looked to be arguing over something by the way Dr. Forrester kept jabbing his finger into the hotel owner's chest.

Taking the opportunity to observe them, she slowed her pace and contemplated their differences. While Mr. Porter was attractive with his wavy brown hair perpetually looking tousled as if he'd stepped in from a high wind, she found to her consternation that she preferred the doctor's darker looks. He exuded a mysterious aura that made her curious to uncover his secrets. A fact, she was sure he would not appreciate. A grin formed, lightening her mood, as she considered what his reaction would be to such questioning into his life. *Denial, probably. Along with a healthy dose of righteous dismissal.*

Lingering longer than she should, she resumed her brisk walk until Mr. Porter spotted her and called her over. "Mrs. Milton! Just who I wanted to see; come join us."

Sparing a glance of longing at the staircase, she dutifully joined them, dipping her head in greeting. "Good evening, gentlemen."

"Mrs. Milton," Dr. Forrester's gruff voice raised the hair on her arms in heightened awareness. She rubbed the feeling away, though she couldn't break their eye contact. It was like sipping a hot toddy as heat curled through her. Bourbon and honey and lemon. She'd yet to see the sweet side of him, but the bitter part of him was alive and well.

"I was just inviting Dr. Forrester to a little soiree I'm having tomorrow night, and I want to invite you as well. It'll be a few of my esteemed guests and friends for a night of conversation or perhaps some parlor games," Mr. Porter said. His grey broadcloth jacket looked positively cheerful next to Dr. Forrester's somber black. Johanna realized she still hadn't seen him in any other color; though men's fashion tended toward the more somber, most men tried to brighten their outfits with touches of color. Not Dr. Forrester it seemed.

As for the party, it had been a while since she'd attended one. Years, in fact, since before her mourning period. Maybe it would be good for her, she thought. It could possibly relieve the dejection she felt at being turned away so often and remind her that she did have a way with people, no matter the losing tallies she marked today.

"That sounds lovely, Mr. Porter. I will let my maid know to prepare one of my gowns worthy of such an event."

"You flatter me," he said, placing a hand over his heart, "I think Dr. Forrester will agree with me when I say, anything you choose to wear will be divine and it's the model that makes the dress."

Most women would titter in excitement to have such a refined man flirting with them, yet Johanna felt nary a flutter, let alone a titter in her stomach or heart. Here was a man near her age, attractive and well-off, just the sort of man she should set her cap for if she wanted to marry and have children in the future. However, his dark counterpart, who stood with his arms crossed over his chest and a scowl wrinkling his face, drew her attention more. *What is wrong with me?*

Dr. Forrester cleared his throat before his dry comment. "Yes, divine like Panacea."

Mr. Porter scratched his cheek and said, "Panacea...Not sure I'm familiar with that one."

Meeting Johanna's gaze, he explained, "She's the goddess of universal remedy or a cure-all for diseases." A fiery ball of embarrassment and anger swirled inside her at the description. Clearly, he thought to insult her suggestion that she could be of some help to him despite her lack of medical knowledge. Tapping her foot against the floor, she forced herself to keep a calm facade as she seethed within.

"Ah, leave it to you to name a goddess having to do with health. I was thinking more Aphrodite or Venus," Mr. Porter grinned at her, but she was too upset to respond to his compliment.

Scoffing, the doctor pointed out. "They're the same person. Aphrodite, Venus. Both the goddess of love and beauty. The least you could do is choose someone more interesting like Artemis."

"Goddess of the hunt and wild nature; I could see that." Someone called for Mr. Porter from the concierge, interrupting them. "Well, as illuminating as this conversation is, it seems I'm needed elsewhere. I will bid you both adieu until tomorrow evening." He bowed with a grand sweep of his arm before departing and leaving them alone.

I should take his cue, Johanna thought, still annoyed with Dr. Forrester's assessment of her, *before I make a scene*.

PORTER'S PARTY HADN'T sounded the least bit interesting until Mrs. Milton showed up. He supposed an evening in her presence wouldn't exactly be a chore, though the same couldn't be said for her. After all, how could he resist when teasing her gave him a modicum of joy? *Which is in short supply these days.*

"I believe I'll take my leave as well," Mrs. Milton said with a huff. She tipped her head up as she turned to go, but he couldn't resist one last comment.

"That's all you have to say? I must say I'm surprised. Until tomorrow, then, where I'm sure you'll fit right in. You can show off those people skills you've been touting."

It was like watching a volcano erupt. She stood still, her back rigid, and he wondered if she'd respond, before she whipped around fire blazing in her eyes and let loose.

"You're right, my strength lies in speaking with people, having civil conversations. Something I'm sure you struggle with. Perhaps I could teach you how to properly behave in mixed company!"

Damn, she was a sight! With her red hair and a hot flush creeping up her neck, her temper shifted something inside him. He wanted to play with her fire.

"And, here, I thought you preferred the role of my student," he drawled as his gaze dropped to her mouth. Pretty with a full bottom lip, he imagined how it would feel under his. A sharp inhale came from her; he assumed she caught his intimate meaning. *Oh, to be that breath.* To be taken inside her, to warm himself by her flame...*Envious of a fucking breath.*

"I...You..." She stumbled over her words. Somehow, they'd moved closer to each other, the air practically steaming between them. It was as if they'd disappeared into their own little world until the hum of conversations popped their bubble. Mrs. Milton must have realized it at the exact moment he did because she took a quick step back and almost tripped over the hem of her gown. Smoothing her hands down her front, she avoided his gaze before saying, "Like I said: I must go. Good evening, sir."

This time he let her go without a word. He needed to get his own emotions under control because whatever was brewing between the two of them couldn't be good. His life had enough problems; no need to add love into the mix. *Love? Who said anything about love? This is desire. Plain and simple.*

Rubbing a weary hand over his cheek, he followed Mrs. Milton's lead. Time to return to his own suite and update his patients' records like he did every night. A task that paled in comparison to the brightness of a certain widow.

AS SOON AS JOHANNA stepped into Mr. Porter's salon, a sense of familiarity calmed her nerves. Men and women stood scattered around the room, decked out in colorful silk gowns and neutral-toned suits, the ebb and flow of conversation restoring some of the confidence she'd lost after another failed day of searching for a job. At least here she knew she had something to offer.

"Mrs. Milton, I'm glad you could join us. Have you met Mr. and Mrs. Winston?" Mr. Porter approached with an older couple trailing behind. Smiling as her old cloak of armor fell comfortably about her shoulders, she launched into an animated discussion over the current season's fashions with Mrs. Winston. For the next few hours, she laughed and traded gossip, feeling lighter than she had in days, until the women rejoined the men after dinner, and she found herself next to Dr. Forrester.

He'd kept to himself most of the evening, despite Mr. Porter's attempts at drawing him into conversations. She almost felt sorry for him but dismissed the emotion; something she did a lot when she was around him. Ever since they'd met, a slew of unwelcome reactions had run amok inside her, from anger to desire to annoyance. The man left quite an impression on her, and she sent up a prayer of thanks that her original plan of assisting him hadn't panned out.

Who knew what would happen between them if they were forced to work in close quarters?

"I see you've been enjoying yourself, Mrs. Milton. I trust you've given up the ridiculous notion of working for me; you seem right at home in this environment. Best to stick with what you know," Dr. Forrester said as he sidled closer to her. His hands were in his pockets as he leaned against the wall covered by a floral design.

"Have no fear. I've, indeed, moved past that ill-advised plan; I've decided to set my cap on a position at a modiste's, providing fashion feedback to patrons." At least that was the plan.

"And how is that coming along?"

She considered lying to save her pride, but what did it matter if he knew the truth? He already thought poorly of her. "If you must know, it hasn't gone well. But it's still early days; I'm confident I'll find something soon."

"You mean no one will have you?" He surveyed the room as they spoke side by side. The crowd had thinned, but two large groups remained towards the center of the room. "And here I thought you had the gift of making connections. Isn't that why you thought you could help me?"

She blanched at the snide comment. At her silence, he faced her and must have noticed how pale she looked. "I'm sorry; I didn't mean?"

"No, you're right. I suppose it was foolish of me to believe I could be anything more than a talking hen at parties. You won't be bothered again by my silly request."

"What request? What are the two of you whispering about over here?" Mr. Porter interrupted them, a twinkle in his eyes, curbing the initial gratitude Johanna felt at his arrival.

"It's nothing," Robert said. His dark eyes didn't leave her as she put some distance between them. Once again, without her realizing, they'd swayed closer to one another like magnets drawn to each other.

"Didn't sound like nothing; in fact, it looked quite heated."

"I'd asked Dr. Forrester if he'd care to take me on as an assistant a few days ago. I thought after the incident with Mrs. Wyland, the patients could benefit from a calm presence to distract them from their injuries. However, the doctor, quite rightly, refused me; that's all." The explanation fell out of her as she hoped it would close the subject.

"Now, there's a thought..." Mr. Porter tapped a manicured finger against his mouth while his gaze bounced between them. "That sounds like a good idea, Forrester, unless you object to her being a woman."

"Her sex has no bearing; her lack of education does."

"Well, you can teach her what she needs to know," Mr. Porter countered. "Yes, I like this idea. You could use the help, I'm sure. Mrs. Milton, congratulations, you're hired."

It seemed he was as impetuous as she when it came to acting before thinking. Mr. Porter offered his hand as shock reverberated down her back. What just happened? Holding a gloved hand out, he shook it firmly while relaying the job details. One thing stuck out in the daze that wrapped around her: free room and board?the item that most worried her, taken care of, just like that.

"Wait a minute, you can't just hire her. I have a say in this," Robert said, straightening from his relaxed pose.

"Actually, you don't. You work for me, and now, so does Mrs. Milton. Trust me; this is for the best. It's not like you originally planned to work alone anyhow." A meaningful look passed between the men, one she couldn't decipher, but it made Dr. Forrester stiffen even more as his mouth pressed into a thin line.

For a moment, she considered refusing Mr. Porter's offer, but his promise of a free place to stay stopped her. She could withstand Dr. Forrester's attitude if it meant not being forced to move to a potentially dangerous situation.

No, somehow, she'd make this work. "I'll see you..." Dr. Forrester turned with a huff and left without so much as a by your leave. "Tomorrow," she finished.

Mr. Porter sighed at the rude departure. "Don't worry; he's not as bad as he seems. He's just had a difficult time of it lately, but I have every confidence that you'll bring him around soon enough."

Smiling weakly, she stared out the door the doctor had exited and prayed for strength to make Mr. Porter's prediction come true.

THE NEXT MORNING JOHANNA experienced a sense of deja vu as she waited for Dr. Forrester in the lobby again. He hadn't bothered to relay his schedule the night before, but she assumed he started sometime in the morning and would pass by her on the way to his office.

Mr. Porter had mentioned something about a medical room in the hotel, but he'd been woefully short on details. Like a fish floundering on dry land, she felt unprepared for her first day, and it didn't sit well.

Seeing Dr. Forrester descend the staircase, she met him at the bottom with a hasty "Hello" as he kept walking right past her. *So, that's how it's going to be.* Expelling a rough breath, she hurried after him, surprised to see they were leaving St. James.

"Where are we going? I thought your patients were hotel guests and staff."

"Today's my day in the rookery, so I'm off the clock. Which means you can stop following me." His long legs ate up the sidewalk as her booted heels rapped a mad beat trying to keep up. *Not this again.*

"Dr. Forrester, would you please slow down?"

"Why? I told you: you're not needed today."

"Perhaps if you'd told me your schedule earlier, I wouldn't have joined you. However, I had to guess, so here I am. Ready and willing to help, even if it's just to volunteer." Heavy breaths punctuated her words. At this rate, she'd be getting her daily exercise and needing to have her dresses taken in.

"Suit yourself." He shrugged but continued his current pace. *Like a damned racehorse.* She allowed herself the mental curse as she kept her mouth shut. *Today's going to be a long day.*

Chapter Eight

Robert knocked on Mrs. Jenkins's door before letting himself in, knowing she had trouble walking. An older woman, she lived alone as most of her children had died at a young age, except for her son, Michael. But after his father's death, he'd decided to run off to London and rarely visited his ailing mother.

When Robert had first started taking on a few of Dr. Lane's patients, it had taken some getting used to dealing with male and female civilians. Soldiers were a unique breed, he'd realized, and home care needed a different touch.

"How are you doing today, Bessie?" They didn't stand on formality after his first visit. She spoke plainly and preferred he did the same.

"I'm doin' alright, doc." The rough croak traveled from a ripped chair by an empty fireplace. Though the summer brought warmer weather, the tattered shawl around her shoulders spoke to the chill she felt.

"Where's your fire, Bessie?" He asked as he knelt before her, pulling his stethoscope out of the bag by his side.

"It's June, m'boy! No need fer a blaze this time a'year," she said before a cough wracked her hunched form. Warming the metal chest-piece first, he placed it on her back, cupping her frail shoulder in a comforting gesture as he listened to her lungs.

"True, but sometimes I prefer the cozy warmth of a fire, no matter the time of year." A soft, feminine voice drifted in from the doorway. Mrs. Milton stood with her back to the door before venturing further into the room. For a moment, he'd forgotten she was there.

A scowl formed between his brows at her uninvited presence. What was Porter thinking hiring her? They rubbed together like oil and water, and he didn't need more trouble in his life; he had more than enough.

"Ay, who's there?" Bessie tensed beneath his hand, her heart rate speeding up.

"Mrs. Johanna Milton, ma'am. I apologize for the surprise, but I'm Dr. Forrester's new assistant. I'm here to make sure you remain comfortable as he performs his ministrations. May I join you?" She gestured to a wooden stool at the old woman's feet. Not waiting for an answer, she sat down in a precarious perch as an ominous creak emitted from the worn furniture.

"Wud do ya mean, 'remain comfortable'? You bout to do something painful, doc?" Her worried gaze met his calm one—remarkable, given the fact that he was frustrated at Mrs. Milton's interference causing Bessie to fret.

"Oh, no!" Mrs. Milton jumped in. "Nothing like that; at least, I don't think..." She looked to him for confirmation to which he gave a quick negative response before she went on. "No, no painful practices today. I thought it'd be calming if you had someone to talk to while Dr. Forrester worked, to kind of distract you. If that would be amenable?"

"Don't have much to talk 'bout…" Bessie trailed off; suspicion clear in her voice.

Robert knew this would be a bad idea, but had Johanna listened? Of course, not; the woman was as stubborn as an ox and as persistent as a beaver building a dam. He continued listing animals she reminded him of as he moved to examine Bessie's feet where her toes were affected the most. *Chatty as a chipmunk, fiery as a dragon*, he chuckled at the comparison.

"Just relax, Bessie, while I check your gout. Have you been following my instructions for care?"

He carefully tested Bessie's toes, his new position placing him close to Mrs. Milton, her spicy cinnamon scent a surprise compared to most women's preference for light florals. It would explain why the smell cut through the moldy aroma that usually filled the room.

"Tryin' me best, doc," Bessie grunted at his gentle touch. Unfortunately, he knew her best still probably wouldn't be good enough. She needed help but couldn't afford any. And it didn't seem like she had any friends either based on their previous conversations. It had taken her a while to warm to him; he doubted Mrs. Milton would have much luck.

"We can talk about anything you'd like: family, concerns…favorite food," she interjected with a smile at the last suggestion. "I can even go first; I love lemon kisses. Ever since I was a little girl they've been my favorite. Now, you go." She leaned forward, encouraging the older woman to share.

Bessie thought about it for a moment before naming, "Sheep trotter."

"Oh, I don't believe I've had that before; I'll have to bring some the next time we visit," Mrs. Milton included him in her outrageous statement. Outrageous because she absolutely would not be accompanying him again, and he doubted she could get Chef Le Beau to make such a dish. It was popular among the lower class for its cheapness and likeness to real meat, though there was little of anything resembling meat actually in it. And he would not be subjected to her presence outside what was required of him by Porter.

"Really?" Bessie's eyes lit up at the promise, and he worried for her future disappointment.

Damn Mrs. Milton! What more trouble would she bring him today?

THE AFTERNOON PROGRESSED much as the morning, with Mrs. Milton trailing behind him, asking him various questions while he tried to ignore her...which was damned hard to do. Of course, he took a grim sort of satisfaction in the way she was received from each patient. Wary of a finely-dressed lady, most people kept her at a distance despite her warm, open nature.

"Where are we going next?" she asked as they left his last patient.

"The hotel; I'm finished for the day. You can go wherever you want," he said, annoyed and confused at her persistence to be friendly. All day, she'd taken his attitude in stride, smoothing over rough edges and pressing on as if they were discussing the weather.

A tinkling laugh met his statement, her hand reaching out again to touch his arm. That's another thing: she kept touching him, and it had him on edge.

"You're a hard man, Dr. Forrester...You haven't softened towards me at all, have you?"

On the contrary, a moment of amusement passed through him. The longer he stayed in her presence, the harder he became. It had been hell trying to control his body's response to her while dealing with patients, but once he forced himself to focus on the tasks at hand, he thought he'd handled himself well enough. But now that they were alone...it was a different story entirely.

"I fail to see how I need your help," he settled on saying, knowing the truth would shock her.

"How can you say that? I know the patients weren't quite as welcoming as I'd hoped, but I *was* able to hold your tools for you and apply pressure to Mr. Barge's cut. Admit that I was at least somewhat useful today." She crossed her arms under her chest, drawing his attention to the soft globes.

"I don't have to admit anything." Although she spoke the truth, those were little things that he'd managed before he ever knew her.

"Oh! And Mrs. Barley mentioned that she enjoyed having a woman present during our visit; there's your proof that I'm needed!" She said with a victorious grin.

"What a relief to have someone else affirm your value since you tote your charms readily enough?without evidence to support such claims."

"You're impossible," she sighed with a tug on her sleeve and silence fell between them. The street bustled with businessmen rushing home for dinner and shopkeepers locking up. Soon, dark would fall over the city bringing the nightly fog. That was one perk of having her along, he supposed. Since he finished early, he didn't have to walk home after sunset, though darkness didn't scare him.

No, he lived in it long enough during the war and the remaining years after. It had taken the combined efforts of his mother and Harry to pull him back from falling victim to it multiple times. That reminder sobered him, washing away any amusement he may have felt bickering with Mrs. Milton.

The lit beacon of the St. James gleamed in the dying sunlight like a sparkling jewel in an otherwise dull scene?the sight a welcome respite. Soon, he'd be in his suite, able to shut out the woman beside him.

As they got closer, Robert recognized regimental horses standing in front of the building as a group of military men gathered on the steps leading into the hotel. A cold sweat formed on his skin at the familiar garb. What were they doing here?

Tension knotted his muscles as he tried to stay in control of his body's response, resisting the tide of memories trying to drag him under. It was vital he got to his room soon; he couldn't afford to have such a reaction in public. Doctors needed to be seen as calm, cool, and collected, not a sweating mess of exposed nerves.

"Dr. Forrester?are you alright?" Mrs. Milton's soft voice cut through the buzzing in his ears. He'd forgotten she was here, overcome by his efforts to appear unruffled.

"I'm fine," he said, choking out the two words.

"Are you sure? You look as if you've seen a ghost."

She wasn't far off; he felt like a specter of the war stood before him in the form of the talking soldiers. But he hadn't realized he could be read so easily; he didn't like it.

Taking a deep breath, he began counting to one hundred in his head again, trying to visualize the numbers and praying it would make quick work of this damned tension.

"It's nothing; I'm just ready to get inside for dinner." He deflected her question and rushed past the troop to enter the lobby. It seemed Mrs. Milton had finally adjusted to his rapid pace as she followed by his side up the staircase.

"I don't believe you. One minute we were walking, then you froze. I didn't notice anything out of place, just the military regiment. But why would that upset you?" Her questions pierced his failing defenses, arrows finding their mark, her curiosity wearing on him.

"It's none of your damn business; you don't know me," he snapped. His medical bag almost slipped out of his sweaty grip as he clenched and unclenched his fist. Johanna reached forward to catch it, her sudden movement almost making him trip as he reeled away from her. The woman was relentless, and he was reaching the end of his rope.

"So, it *was* the troop..." she concluded, going on as if he hadn't just told her to mind her own business, once again ignoring his wishes. And the stubborn woman thought *him* impossible!

"Do you have some sort of history there?"

He whipped around, backing her into the wall at the top of the stairs, in full view of anyone looking up, but he didn't care. He'd had enough. "I said it's none of your business," he growled, punctuating each word by inching closer to her until he was a hair's breadth away.

Brown eyes stared up into his glare, her accelerated heartbeat evident in the rampant pulsing at her neck. That cinnamon scent teased him again, the fiery aroma matching her wild red hair. Dropping his eyes to her mouth, he wondered if her taste would match.

Quick puffs of air fell from her slightly parted lips, and he couldn't hold himself back any longer. His restraint had tested the limits all day, and now with an attack riding him hard, it was completely broken.

Gripping her neck, he dragged her up to meet his rough kiss. He felt her stiffen in shock at the contact, but he pressed forward, licking around the seam of her lips before dipping inside to taste. Surprise flitted through him as her reaction seemed untried, which was impossible considering she'd been married. But the innocence in her shy responses couldn't be denied. *Or maybe she isn't accustomed to being accosted in public*, the wry comment rose to the surface of his addled-brain.

Her small hands came up to his shoulders where he felt the pinpricks of her nails dig in before a low moan fluttered through her chest. Encouraged, he deepened the kiss, leaning further into her. Spicy warmth met his advances and reminded him of Christmases spent in front of the fire with mulled cider. Burning ribbons of silk wrapped around him, drawing him closer to her body, desperate to be bound by her, to have any form of control exerted over his careening senses.

JOHANNA WASN'T SURE what had happened: one moment they were talking, and the next Dr. Forrester had her pushed against the wall with his mouth devouring hers.

Howard had never kissed her like this; in fact, they'd hardly kissed at all. He preferred completing his marital duty as quickly as possible before leaving her alone in her bed. And once he realized she would not be providing sons for him, even that came to stop as he cut a swath through London in a desperate attempt to sire an heir to continue his legacy.

She heard of his exploits through the gossip grapevine, and while it hurt to know her husband was being so promiscuous, she found the majority of her pain stemmed from her inability to have children. She'd never developed significant feelings for Howard, but the fact that she may be barren cut deep.

The scratch of Robert's whiskers against her smooth skin interrupted the maudlin thoughts, his earlier clean-shaven jaw covered in new growth. Like champagne bubbles, emotions fizzed around inside her: curiosity, frustration, excitement...desire.

The last awed her with its ferocity. She'd never understood the few conversations overheard at parties of married women detailing their extramarital exploits. She always wondered what led these women, and indeed their husbands, to cheat on their spouse for a night of passion with someone else. She knew it was a usual, and almost expected, occurrence between married couples, but it confounded her, the blatant flouting of vows and no care for promises made.

Now, as Robert's kiss sent her reeling into some unknown euphoria, she finally felt an inkling of understanding. Passion such as this would be undeniably enticing for a spouse stuck in a loveless marriage with a disinterested partner.

She tentatively matched his movements, her tongue gliding along his, eliciting a rough groan of encouragement from him. The power of bringing this man pleasure lit her up inside like a flower drawing energy from the sun. Emboldened, she moved her hands up to his wavy hair, tousling the dark strands as she pulled him closer.

"Johanna," his stuttered whisper, her name said in such a desperate way, brought a sense of contentment that felt out of place during a passionate embrace. The utterance embodied a deep pain and spoke of his need for comfort with desire mixing in to form an irresistible elixir for Johanna's tender heart.

"Robert..." She dared to say his name in return. It amazed her that they were strangers, yet she felt this connection to him, one that had grown each time they'd met, and even today as she'd watched him with patient after patient.

Despite her implications that he intimidated those he looked after, he'd proved her wrong with each gentle touch and kind word, caring for the poor and unwell with admirable aplomb. Though his demeanor hadn't thawed towards her, she'd seen the warm, affectionate man he could be, the one who made her feel this undeniable heat now as he retreated to pepper kisses over her cheek and neck.

His hand on her waist began an upward ascent until a crash below jerked them apart. A moment passed as they stood frozen staring into each other's eyes, trying to decipher their confusing feelings.

Robert broke first. Dropping his hands to fidget at his side, he rubbed his fingers together in open and closed fists revealing his agitation. Noticing his fallen medical bag, he reached down to pick it up, holding it in front of him like a talisman to ward off any advances she might make.

"I apologize." He rubbed a shaky hand down his pant leg, avoiding eye contact, "I'm not myself tonight; I'll take my leave now. Good evening." He gave a short bow before practically sprinting down the hallway to his room. She remained behind, standing limp against the wall at her back, overlooking the marble railing separating her from the floor below.

A few parties passed casting sidelong glances her way as she contemplated the events of the day. It was fortunate that they hadn't been near thirty seconds earlier. They certainly would've gotten an eyeful?along with ruining her reputation, she thought with a frown. Now that clear thinking was returning to her tingling form, she couldn't believe what she'd done. Hills and valleys had marked the day; one moment she was scaling a mountain peak and the next, she'd been knocked down to the very lowest of points.

So much had happened, she could hardly fathom it. And while Robert's kiss rose as the highlight, it also shared the honor of being the most intriguing, as it was precipitated by such an abnormal reaction to the soldiers outside. What had set him off?

She considered speaking with Mr. Porter to see if he could enlighten her, though as a man privy to many guests' secrets, she wondered how forthcoming he'd be. Sighing, she straightened her dress and retired to her suite—nothing would be resolved that night.

But she would learn more about the mysterious Dr. Forrester, starting tomorrow when she joined him again, determined now to help him in all ways: professional and personal.

Chapter Nine

L oud booms shook the ground beneath him as two men placed their injured comrade on his makeshift surgery table before heading back into the fray outside. The stoic soldier clutched a bleeding arm to his chest, and though fortunate enough to still be alive, the bullet wound would cost him a limb as Robert eyed the torn ligaments and bone. Raising his voice above the chaos happening around him, he called to Harry, asking for anything to make the amputation more bearable.

"There's no more, Rob," Harry said, a grim look in his eyes. He turned back to tying off the last stitch on a man who'd gotten cut by a piece of flying shrapnel.

"Already?" He knew camp rations were running low, but he'd prayed it wouldn't come to this...again. It was hard enough treating all the sick soldiers with limited supplies, but it was worse when he was left no choice but to saw through a man's bone while conscious. Sick dread welled inside him at what he'd have to do.

"I'm sorry; I used the last of it earlier with Corporal Lansing." He indicated the bed in the corner where the soldier lay quiet. Casting a worried glance over Robert's patient, his resigned face showed that he knew what this meant.

Robert's head hung low as he closed his eyes in defeat. But he knew they couldn't wait any longer and turned to the soldier. "I *won't sugarcoat it; this is going to hurt, but it's the only way you'll have a chance to survive."*

"I understand, doc."

Releasing a long exhale, Robert placed a strip of leather between the soldier's teeth before securing his body to the table with frayed bands of linen, knowing the pain of the saw would make it impossible for the man to remain still.

Once everything was set, Robert picked up the curved saw, cleaned as best he could in these circumstances, and took another deep breath. He sent up a prayer that the soldier would pass out quickly, but just as he was about to start, Harry called out, "Wait! I have an idea."

Walking over, he uttered an apology to the soldier, then knocked the man out with a swift punch.

"Are you out of your mind? We can't afford injuring your hand."

Harry backed away, lifting his hands in appeasement. "It's done. You better hurry up before he wakes up again."

A shudder of relief coursed through Robert as he looked down at the unconscious man and released a tightly-held breath. "Thank you; now, see to your own patient. I can handle this."

Fear jolted Robert awake as the memory echoed in his head. Sitting up, his gaze skittered around the room, eventually recognizing he was home — not on a battlefield. The bedsheets clung to his clammy skin, and the adrenaline of another nightmare coursed through his blood. They were coming more frequently now; he doubted he got more than a few hours of sleep each night.

Groaning, he banged his fists against the mattress beneath him. *Damn, this fucking miserable life!* He wanted to curse his mother and Harry for dying but couldn't bring himself to utter the words. It wasn't their fault, that without them, he couldn't handle his memories anymore.

He missed the way his mother would comfort him with soothing murmurs and baked treats, always encouraging him to continue living life, that he wasn't an irredeemable, damaged mess. And Harry always had a way to brighten his mood whether by practical jokes or tricks to curb his mind when he started spinning out of control.

Now, he didn't have either of them?both gone in such quick succession. It felt like a one-two punch whose effects were catching up and threatening to knock him out.

Getting out of bed, he walked out to the sitting room, uncapped a bottle of whiskey, and took a deep gulp. He willed the alcohol to burn away the painful memories. As was quickly becoming his ritual, after that first generous swig, he dropped to the floor and began completing push-ups before moving on to sit-ups, the repetitive exercises soothing some of his tension.

Muted daylight crept in a while later announcing it was time to get ready for the day. When a maid arrived with breakfast, he sat washed and dressed at the dining table, going over his list of patients to see that day. He wondered if Mrs. Milton would dare to join him again after their kiss. He'd lost control last night as if he'd been back on the war field again, only this time being pelted by Mrs. Milton's questions. If the woman had any sense, she'd stay far away. And if that thought caused a pique of discontentment, he ignored it.

A quarter of an hour later, he strode down the marble staircase to find Johanna waiting for him in the same spot as yesterday. It could have been a replica except she'd traded the serviceable grey dress for a brighter green one, the color highlighting the light brown of her eyes.

"You're back." Exasperation coated the short statement, while an unwanted sliver of excitement at seeing her again tried to poke its head up.

"Surely, you didn't think one little kiss would scare me off?" she said. A cheeky smile transformed her pretty face and sent a shiver of awareness through him.

"I'd hoped you'd have more sense. Clearly, I gave you too much credit." He stepped around her, a feeling of deja vu hitting him. He couldn't afford distractions today. Lack of sleep and the aftereffects of his attack from yesterday combined to make him extra irritable; it took all of his willpower to focus on the day ahead. People's well-being was in his care, so he didn't need Johanna whittling away at his already raw nerves.

"Oh, Dr. Forrester, how you do say the nicest things. Truly...such a charmer." She rolled her eyes as they walked down the corridor to his office. The lush carpet muffled their footfalls and made the hallway feel cocoon-like in its silence. Robert wondered if Porter deliberately put him towards the back of the building because of its distance from the commotion at the heart of the hotel. Even employees were a rare sight unless they intentionally came to visit him.

"If you want charm, go find Mr. Porter," he suggested even as a part of him balked at sending her in another man's direction.

"As amiable as Mr. Porter is, I prefer the company of your patients. Who are we seeing first?" she asked. A spurt of unwarranted pleasure shot through him at her choice to stay. He really must be out of sorts. She'd been refusing to leave him alone since the moment he met her; it shouldn't surprise him that she wouldn't give up now.

But if he had to be stuck with a companion, he could do worse than a beautiful young woman.

Chapter Ten

A few weeks passed as they developed a routine. Every morning she waited for Dr. Forrester, and slowly his visual response shifted from annoyance to acceptance. *If only his patients felt the same way.*

Despite her assurances to him about her skill at making people feel at ease and get them talking, thus distracting them from whatever task he was performing, she was having trouble. As she accompanied him on his usual rounds, only a few people had welcomed her presence.

They saw three types of patients: the hotel staff, the hotel guests who requested a visit, and those who lived in the rookeries under Dr. Lane's care. She had better luck with the guests, who felt comfortable speaking with someone of their status as Dr. Forrester looked them over. However, the employees were tentative and unsure of how to respond to a lady when the topic didn't revolve around her next cup of tea. But the most suspicious of everyone were the poor souls in Devil's Haven.

Most still looked askance at her, no matter how much she tried to ease their qualms. In fact, sometimes she worried she was making their doctor's visits harder by being there. But of all the patients they saw, they were the ones she was most curious about. The few stories she'd heard fascinated Johanna since she'd lived a fairly sheltered life despite growing up in London.

From a well-to-do family, all she'd seen had been society luncheons and galas. As the daughter of a baron, she never could have imagined some of the horrors she learned about. So even though her original plan of making people feel more comfortable was failing, she was gaining an education on the perils the lower class faced along with a medical one.

It seemed her fanciful first idea of speaking to calm patients needed to make way for a more practical way of aiding Robert, she'd concluded.

He required someone to hold certain instruments or apply pressure to wounds?more than a talkative companion. And though she'd hesitated taking on such tasks in the beginning, feeling vastly unqualified, she kept reminding herself that she'd barged her way into his life and practice to help?even if that help took on a different form than she'd envisioned.

Each new day made her more determined to stick with Dr. Forrester and assist as many people as she could. She woke every morning with purpose; something that had always eluded her before. Now if only she could figure out the rest of her life, like possibly remarrying and starting a family. A frown wrinkled her brow, though, as that would mean she'd have to quit her current job. *No need to fret now; that's a problem for future Johanna.*

Tilting her head, she studied Dr. Forrester as they returned to the St. James. As a physician, she assumed he would have that same sense of fulfillment from helping people all the time, but his stoic demeanor never betrayed any buoyant emotion such as happiness or contentment. No, she had the distinct impression that he was the exact opposite of those things most of the time.

He put up a good front with patients, always warm and understanding, which jarred her when she considered his usual attitude with her. But once they left someone's home, he reverted to his unhappy self.

She'd tried approaching Mr. Porter on the topic, but he'd directed her to ask the man himself if she wanted to know his secrets. His refusal had been somewhat of a surprise. With such a carefree persona like every other social butterfly she'd known, she figured he'd love to gossip. But his loyalty to his friend and employee had stood strong against her queries.

Shadows played over Dr. Forrester's harsh features as the light faded. This was the latest they'd been out, but they'd had a difficult case with Bessie. Her gout wasn't improving, so he'd given her a stern talking to that did not go over well with the older woman. Their back and forth had gone on despite Johanna's attempts to defuse the situation.

"Eyes forward," Robert ordered her as they passed under a gaslight being lit for the evening hours.

"How do you know they're not?"

"Because I can feel you staring at me. Your gaze is like a hot poker; it burns me." The admission shocked her. After their kiss all those weeks ago, they'd settled into a companionable partnership, ignoring any sort of passionate desires. To be honest, it had left her feeling something akin to disappointment. Which was ridiculous considering her experience with men.

However, after such a shocking yet pleasurable embrace, a part of her had yearned for more. Howard had never made her blood race or sent sparks of sensation to her most private of places. No, he'd spent little time wooing her, preferring to get his duty over quickly as she lay still beneath him.

Many widows took lovers after their husbands died as they were no longer bound by the strict rules set for unmarried women; it was almost expected, if not spoken of aloud. But she'd never felt any inclination to participate in such bed sport; Howard had seen to that. Now, though, she considered the potential pleasure to be had as she glanced over at Robert again. Flashes of him over her, his clean-shaven face shining with a gleam of sweat as he thrust...

"You're doing it again." He pulled her to the side, his rigid jaw revealing the tension in his body. "You won't like where it leads you." His husky warning sent tingles down her spine and heightened her curiosity.

The faintest glow from a streetlight glanced over his face before solid brick met her back as they moved deeper into the dark alley. *Not the most romantic of spots*...One of his hands landed above her shoulder as he leaned over her, bringing the briefest whiff of sandalwood, immediately distracting her.

Another hand curled around her waist and drew her closer to him where a hard ridge dug into her belly; his arousal clear. Excitement fluttered in her veins as butterflies took flight in her tightly laced stomach.

"Don't presume to know what I like," she countered in an unrecognizably sultry voice that surprised her. Never had she heard such a tone come from her mouth; there hadn't been much need before. But now, in the presence of this man, she welcomed the discovery.

Robert drew his cheek along hers, the roughened skin within a whisper of touching. Warm breath at her ear caused a trembling down her spine as he whispered, "Are you saying you want me to pin you against this wall and have my wicked way with you? Kiss those soft red lips? Bite that sweet..."

She covered his mouth with her hand, breathless as she imagined him performing such indecent but intriguing acts. "I quite understand your meaning, sir." The proper words fell from her out of habit until she continued, decidedly improper, "And yes, that's what I want."

His dark eyes widened at her scandalous response and a coil of satisfaction from shaking the impenetrable Dr. Forrester's composure settled in her. Noises from the street, only a few feet beyond them, drifted into the alley as people and carriages passed completely unaware of the sexual tension rising so close to them.

"So be it," he muttered, the heat from his breath penetrating her gloved hand before he shifted to cover her mouth with his. This time she eagerly opened for him, inviting a deeper kiss, desperate to explore this newfound desire.

Rising to her tiptoes, she used his shoulders for balance as she returned his ardor. Mutual groans of pleasure pulsed through the air as their tongues dueled for supremacy. He tasted like the dessert pastry they shared for a snack a few hours earlier: tart apple delighting her taste buds. The addictive flavor branded into her brain; she would never view apples the same way again. *Or alleyways. Or handsome, brusque doctors...*

"Johanna...god..." His mouth broke away on a gasp before trailing down until the high collar of her dress prevented him from reaching bare skin. "I want to mark you right here." He bit down gently on the spot where her neck and shoulder met, wetting the fabric and sending a visceral response down between her thighs. Unsteady, she dug her nails into his shoulders and taunted, the words coming from some deep, hidden well, "Only if I get the same privilege."

The bold act of aggression amazed her along with a sense of overwhelming possessiveness. She wanted Robert, and she alone wanted to have him, anyway she could: married or not. Like a bolt of lightning, it struck her that she would take this man into her bed, and she didn't care what such a thing said about her. Morals bedamned!

One moment she'd been living her life, finding her way in the world, and now she had this jolt of awareness as Robert held her in his arms.

"Who are you, and what have you done with proper Johanna?" The wonder on his face shone in the muted light. She could explain how proper Johanna was alive and well but was letting her spontaneous sister have some fun. Or maybe tell him that she was finished with society's rules, finally stepping into the freedom of her widowhood. A hundred thoughts flashed through her mind, but only one clamored the loudest. "This *is* me; just Johanna."

And it was true. A giddy lightness filled her as she threw off the chains the world had placed on her; it felt like a weight had been lifted off her shoulders as she stood taller. No one was forcing her to act a certain way anymore, telling her what she should or shouldn't be doing; her working with Robert proved that true. He accepted and wanted her as she was, even when she frustrated him with her bubbly sometimes pushy personality. A happy smile spread over her face at the realization.

He studied her for a minute longer, and she wondered if he could sense the change in her. Placing a soft kiss on her forehead, he stepped back, extricating himself from her embrace.

"I'm not sure you can ever be *just Johanna*..." He tapered off before a teasing glint entered his eyes. "You can be *jovial Johanna* or *ginger Johanna*." He motioned to her red hair. "But the word *just* implies a simplicity or dullness that we both know is false."

The compliment warmed her as he guided her back to the sidewalk. The only concession to their previous embrace was his arm looped through hers.

"Well, thank you," she said, blushing. "Though I feel like I should take offense at the ginger comment. I'm more of a dark auburn; no orange in sight." She patted her hair as if to reassure herself.

"Lord save me," he sighed as she launched into an explanation of the difference in colors. With her hand resting on his forearm, they looked like any other couple strolling through the night air, having an entertaining discussion.

And she imagined what it would be like if they were married, able to touch and converse whenever they wanted to—the joy of having someone to share life with, unlike her previous union. *Don't get ahead of yourself; it's only a kiss.*

But the notion caused her heart to beat a bit faster as she blinked away an unexpected rush of tears. What would that sort of life be like?

Chapter Eleven

A knock at the door disturbed Robert's reading of the latest article published by Joseph Lister on germ theory. Glancing at the clock, he wondered who would bother him at this time of night; most people had left for their evening engagements by now. Annoyed, he walked to the door and opened it to find Porter standing with a coaxing grin on his face. Robert knew this didn't bode well for the quiet night at home he'd planned.

Porter barged in, taking in the luxurious suite and nodding in approval at his handiwork, "This is a damn good room...Don't say I never did anything for you."

"What do you want, Porter?" He cut straight to the point. Every so often, he would drop by unannounced to encourage Robert to join him on some sort of jaunt about town. Something about his need to get out more and have fun. He knew he never should've agreed to Porter's club that one night; now the man was more determined than ever.

"Is that any way to greet a friend?" He placed a hand over his wounded heart, failing miserably to earn any sympathy from him. He knew the man's game.

"I don't recall hearing a greeting, just you bragging about the hotel you built. So, I'll ask again: what do you want?"

"I thought you might like to join me at the club tonight; take a break from your whole work then home hermit routine," Porter passed a hand over the fireplace mantel before rubbing his fingers together as they came away with traces of grime. "I'll speak with Mrs. Moore about the maids. They need to spend a little more time here." The absent-minded comment was followed by a shake of the curtains to test for dust motes.

Robert made no reply, instead focusing on Porter's first statement. "I'm perfectly content with my current routine; I don't need to go to a smoke-filled gentleman's club full of dandies or old men."

"Come now, there's more to it than that," Porter said. "We have our fair share of rakes and curmudgeons as well. It'll be fun which you are in sore need of...unless you have a previous engagement?" A taunting glimmer formed in his eyes as Robert became warier of the turn of conversation.

"Of course not," he refuted; he never had engagements—previous or otherwise. Porter tapped the wooden side table set against the settee, a curious humming coming from him.

"Really? I figured with as much time as you and Mrs. Milton were spending together, you might be mixing business with pleasure. And I'll admit that was part of my reasoning for hiring her to help you. You need a woman to help loosen you up."

"It's not like that between us," he lied, remembering their kiss from earlier that night. She'd shocked him with her eagerness and acceptance of his advances. He'd never met a woman like her: a prim and proper butterfly with a wild, rebellious side. The two parts of her melded together into one intriguing woman he was finding difficult to resist. "Besides she's a lady.

She accompanies me on doctor visits and assists with patients; nothing more."

Although she helped *him* more than the people they saw. It was challenging to gain their trust, especially by a woman like Johanna. Yet, he had no doubt she'd wear them down eventually?as she'd done with him. No, for now, it was useful having an extra pair of hands around to pass him tools or hold a bandage.

But it was more than that. Against his better judgment, he found he enjoyed having her along despite his early misgivings. She reminded him of a hummingbird; like the bird's wings, her chatter hardly missed a beat as her mind constantly came up with new questions to ask. A chaotic energy surrounded her that somehow drew him in. *Or, perhaps, it's simply lust.* Maybe he needed to exorcise her from his mind with a good fucking...and after her actions earlier, she might even let him.

"Right...which is why she questioned me about your past and possible time spent in the military," Porter said. Well, that brought him back to reality. Nothing like the mention of the military to douse any lingering desire. Porter crossed one booted leg over the other as he took a seat before continuing, "I got the distinct impression that there was more than professional interest there."

This was the first he'd heard of Johanna's inquisition, though it didn't surprise him, he'd shut down her attempts to interrogate him about his past. It was only natural that she'd move onto a new source. As someone privy to guests' information, Porter would be able to provide insight into him.

"And what did you tell her?" Robert asked.

"Don't worry; I kept your secrets. The little I know of them anyway...You're a damned locked box, you know that?"

Relief coursed through him at Porter's silence. And it would explain why Johanna hadn't brought the subject up in their conversations. "Thank you, and I don't prefer to broadcast my personal life unlike you." His barbed statement hit its mark, but Porter shrugged, fully acknowledging his open demeanor.

"I guess that means you haven't told her about Dr. Rosing, yet, either?" He pushed, a somber look in his eyes. Returning to the article he'd been reading, Robert tried focusing on the sentences crossing the page.

"No."

"Don't you think it might be helpful to speak with someone about it? I know it's still recent, but you hole yourself up here like a widow in mourning. He was your best friend; I doubt he'd want you to live life this way," Porter urged.

"What do you know about Harry? So, we drank a couple of times together; that doesn't make you an expert," he scoffed. The table beneath him shook as his bobbing knee bumped it. Steadying it, he made a conscious effort to still the agitated movement. Which was difficult with Porter bringing up things he didn't want to talk about.

"Maybe not. But he seemed a sociable sort of man, and without him, you've become one of those curmudgeons I mentioned earlier. I'm not going to let you waste away alone in this room when we can go out. You need a friend, and I'm volunteering."

Slapping his hands against his thighs, Porter stood and demanded, "Now, let's get going. Play a couple of hands of poker, drink a few glasses of whiskey, and I'll call the night a success.

Then you'll be free to return here to your...work." He motioned to the papers sitting on the small writing desk.

"Or I can stay here and not waste my time with trivial pursuits."

Porter studied his stern posture, eyes narrowed, and arms crossed over his chest, and mimicked the stance. "I'm not taking 'no' for an answer."

God save him from stubborn people! Robert released a frustrated breath as he got up and gathered his coat and hat. First, Johanna wouldn't leave him alone, and now Porter seemed to be stealing a page from her book.

"Lead the way," he dropped in a mocking bow.

Straightening his jacket, Porter consoled, "Cheer up, one of these days you'll thank me for this. We're going to be great friends, you'll see." And with a charming grin and pat on Robert's back, he led them to their destination.

Robert shook his head at the prediction; he didn't understand Porter's persistence. The man must have plenty of friends with his personality. Why did he feel the push to add Robert to that long list? It reminded him of a certain woman who poked and prodded his defenses, determined to barge in and wreck his guarded life. Just like Johanna, Porter didn't know when to leave well enough alone?the two of them should form a club.

Because if there was one thing he knew, that rang clear through his head and heart: he needed to be alone, never risking someone learning of his troubled mind.

Chapter Twelve

The sound of children playing upstairs drifted down to the parlor where Johanna and Ava sat drinking their afternoon tea. Loud thumps followed by squeals of laughter attested to an exciting playtime after returning from the Sunday church service an hour ago. Clearly, it was time for all their pent-up energy to be released.

"It seems Nanny is having a tough time of it." Ava cast a worried glance heavenward. A frown marred her pale face, replacing her usual pleasant expression.

"Oh, let them have their fun," Johanna said softly, a tinge of pain in her heart at the lack of such happy sounds in her own life. *Maybe someday.*

"I don't mind a little roughhousing," Ava explained, "But when it feels like they're trying to shake the roof off the house, I get a little concerned…" Another boom went off punctuating her statement.

"They're fine, dear. Now, I must tell you about my new venture with Dr. Forrester." Johanna smoothly changed the subject, having been dying to tell her best friend about her work with Robert. Aside from short letters, they hadn't found time to chat until that afternoon. And a tremor of guilt went through her at the realization. She'd come to Manchester to visit Ava, yet she'd abandoned her to pursue a new adventure with Robert. She would need to make more of an effort to balance the two worlds.

"Yes! I'm quite intrigued; I know you were searching for something to fill your time, but this seems a bit extreme."

"Nonsense! This is exactly what I should be doing. It's just like your charity boards except I'm skipping the middleman and going directly to the people who need the most help." Johanna leaned forward, setting her teacup on the table in front of her. Excitement radiated from her pores; she wanted Ava to understand the importance of her work.

"While that sounds lovely, are you sure it's safe?" Ava asked before taking a slow sip of tea as her brows furrowed in worry.

Johanna waved her hand. "Of course! Robert...I mean Dr. Forrester, would never commit any unwelcome advances." Which was true, she supposed, as any advances from him were quite welcome and encouraged. But she didn't tell Ava that, at least not yet.

"I wasn't speaking of Dr. Forrester," Ava drawled, filing Johanna's familiarity with his name away for future discussion. "I meant mingling with the poor diseased class of Manchester. I'm not sure how safe it is. What if you catch something horrible?"

The blatant elitism stunned Johanna for a moment before she recovered sufficiently to respond,

"Why, Ava Lynn Jensen, since when did you become so heartless? A rich man is just as susceptible to disease as a poor one, and I should know because I help with *those* guests at the hotel. The only difference is the former can afford healthcare whereas these people cannot. They need our help, and if Robert's willing to risk himself, so can I. Besides, we mostly deal with bumps and bruises or chronic illnesses that aren't catching." Johanna ended her tirade with a huff, righteous anger burning through her veins, her rare temper revealing itself.

Ava appeared suitably chastened as her head ducked in shame, a red blush spreading on her cheeks. Instant compassion replaced Johanna's ire as she continued softly, "I don't mean to be insulting, but I think, as the caring woman you are, a woman who serves on charity organizations and raises funds to help these same people, you should show more empathy and understanding. If not for our good fortune at birth, we might very well be in their position."

"You're right," Ava said, reaching over to place a placating hand on Johanna's arm. "I just worry about you. It's been marvelous having you close after you've been away for so long; I don't want to lose you."

Johanna understood her apprehension; it was difficult finding true friends in their social circles. Everyone lived by a set of rules and pretense, making it nearly impossible to build real friendships. They were fortunate enough to have found each other at a young age and always have that support. A question of who supported Robert popped into her head, as it occurred to her that she'd never seen him with anyone outside his work.

But she shook off the thought to focus on her friend. "I understand, and I feel the same way. Just trust that I'm being as careful as possible. However, I must admit it hasn't gone as I'd planned."

"What do you mean?" Ava asked. She refilled her empty teacup, offering the pot to Johanna.

Shaking her head, Johanna explained, "The people aren't as receptive as I'd hoped. There's a wall between us that I can't seem to overcome."

"Isn't that to be expected? You're the daughter of a baron, and they're common people," Ava raised a hand in defense. "And I don't mean that in a belittling way, just stating a fact. It's natural for them to be wary of you. Besides, not everyone feels comfortable opening up to strangers." She shot a pointed look at Johanna, since once upon a time she'd been one of those people.

Johanna sighed, setting her teacup and saucer down, before flopping back into her seat. "You're right. I just had such high hopes of stepping in and comforting patients like I did for Mrs. Wyland?using my incessant talking for something good." Dejection set in as she remembered their last patient visit the day before. As hard as she'd tried to be engaging, the taciturn man had refused to open up.

"Hey," Ava's soft voice called to her. "Don't give up yet. You haven't been at this for very long; it takes time to build trust. And your social skills have already done a lot of good. I know Howard didn't appreciate you as he should have, and he was wrong for it."

They exchanged a quiet look of support at the mention of her former husband. Ava knew all about the troubles in their marriage and had supported her through everything.

"Alright; enough of that." Johanna clapped her hands in exclamation, trying to shake off the air of melancholy that had settled over them. "Can we move on from such maudlin talk to discuss the interesting altercation I had with Dr. Forrester? I have so much to share!"

An interested light twinkled in Ava's eyes as she sat forward, "Yes! I've been dying to hear what it's like to work with *Robert*." She stressed his name, recalling Johanna's familiar use of the moniker.

Johanna laughed at her friend's eagerness, happy to leave behind talk of her husband and her shortcomings, "Well, he's a bit of a mystery. With patients, he's very kind and warm, something I hadn't thought possible after our first meeting. Yet with me, he seems to have mixed emotions. At times, he treats me like a pest hanging onto his coattails, while other times..." She remembered their exhilarating kisses.

"Other times..." Ava prompted, waving her hand for Johanna to continue.

"He's kissed me. Twice," she blurted out. Ava's eyes widened as a quick gasp fell from her lips.

Fanning herself, she questioned, "And how was it?"

A satisfied smile formed on Johanna's face, "Lovely. Unexpected. Passionate." A trail of adjectives flitted through her brain, but those three summed up the experience. "I never knew a kiss could make me feel that way."

"How exciting! You deserve happiness, and it's been years since Howard passed."

"True, but I'm not sure anything will come from this. It's only kissing, after all, not a marriage proposal. I mean, I've known the man for only a few weeks." Yet, she felt a stronger connection with him than she did with Howard after eleven years. *And you've already decided you're willing to bed him.* But she'd keep that last part to herself.

Ava tapped a finger on her pursed lips. "Hmm, that's true. And I'm not sure it's entirely proper for him to be so forward so soon."

"That doesn't bother me," Johanna waved away her concern. "I'm an experienced widow; no need for typical rules?as people keep telling me." No, the speed of their intimacy suited her just fine. She was more worried about what haunted him and caused such a bizarre reaction to the military regiment. But she didn't share that with her friend, yet, either. A compulsion to protect Robert prevented her from elaborating too much on their relationship, even though keeping secrets was unusual for her. An open book, she spoke rashly, speaking before thinking things through, unlike Ava. So, this was a change for her.

"Well, try not to stray too far from the rules," Ava warned. "Now, tell me more about him besides his passionate kisses. And about your visits. I know you haven't had much luck with patients, but I'm sure you've met some interesting characters."

And just like that, they settled into their usual rhythm of Johanna entertaining Ava with wild tales, reconnecting as only true friends can do.

Chapter Thirteen

They decided to break for lunch after seeing Mrs. Jenkins again. Johanna smiled as she recalled how far she'd gotten with the older woman. After initial reticence, she and Bessie had formed a sort of friendship. Bessie was full of interesting stories of growing up in the rookeries, fascinating Johanna with incredible tales of survival. She doubted her own withal to survive some of the circumstances Bessie had.

"How about a ham sandwich?" Robert asked as they came upon a cart on the sidewalk. Agreeing to his suggestion, they purchased their meals before taking a seat on a nearby bench, looking out on the busy thoroughfare.

Thick slices of ham lay between a crusty bread roll, and Johanna eyed it hungrily before taking a bite. The salty sweet flavor exploded on her tongue. For her first experience of street food, it was delicious. "Mmm."

"Don't make that sound," Robert said. Shooting him a confused look, she caught the way his darkened eyes watched her, heat from his implication coursing through her. Ducking her head, she swallowed hard. A few minutes of silence passed as they finished their lunch; passing conversations provided enough background noise to cover the awkward moment.

Pulling out a handkerchief, Johanna wiped her hands before offering it to Robert. He thanked her, and she noticed the

cracking along his palms. It wasn't the first time she'd noticed. As often as he washed his hands to keep them as clean as possible for patients, it was no mystery how his hands became so dry.

Johanna searched through her reticule until she found the small jar of hand cream she carried around. "Here, give me your hand," she ordered as Robert returned the used handkerchief.

Stuffing it in a pocket of her dress, she unscrewed the cap, dipped a finger in to swipe up a dollop of the thick moisturizer, and held a hand out for him.

"Why?" A raised eyebrow accompanied his skeptical tone. He eyed the gelatinous substance as if it was poisonous.

Resisting the urge to laugh at his fear, she said, "Don't worry; trust me."

There was a pause as she stared him down, carriages passing before them letting the rhythmic clip-clop of hooves on cobblestones to filter through. Finally, Robert relented and placed a large hand in her smaller one. A thrill of pleasure at his acquiescence settled in her stomach, fluttering butterfly wings taking flight.

"How long have you lived in Manchester?" she asked, hoping to distract herself from the nervous feeling. She still didn't know much about his past, and curiosity itched beneath her skin.

"About a month," he said. Surprise filtered through her; they must've arrived in town around the same time. It's a wonder they hadn't met sooner. "Not for very long, then. What brought you here?"

Smoothing the cream into his rough hands, she imagined those fingertips running over her skin. The rough pads

stroking...*Focus, Johanna*! Good lord, what was becoming of her? They were sitting outside in broad daylight, yet she couldn't stop the scandalous ideas from surfacing.

He took a while to answer her question as the friction from their hands warmed the salve, the spicy aroma blooming between them. "This is why you always smell like cinnamon."

Startled by his observation, she met his steady gaze. "Yes, I suppose it is," she said, resuming massaging his hand. "This is one of my favorite creams. I also have the distilled bath oil, too."

"Of course," he chuckled. It was the first time she'd heard him laugh, and the sound sent those pesky butterflies off again.

Smiling, she shrugged, "I like these natural lotions and oils. A few years ago, I discovered a woman in Derbyshire that made them from ingredients in her garden. I've been hooked ever since."

"Sounds better than some of the women's products peddled out there."

"Agreed. I've had some horrible reactions to certain creams before." Gesturing for him to switch hands, she rubbed another dollop of cream into the cracked skin. "But enough about me. You were telling me what brought you to town."

Sighing, he stared out at the food vendor as he sold more sandwiches to hungry travelers.

"You're relentless, you know that?"

"I've heard something like that a time or two," she admitted?mostly from him.

"I moved here with a friend and colleague, Harry. We preferred the smaller city life compared to London, and he thought there might be more of a need for physicians here with the factory workers."

This was the first Johanna had heard of a friend, but it made her happy to know he wasn't completely alone. She'd spent more time than she cared to admit wondering about the relationships in his life.

"And where is Harry now? I haven't seen him around the hotel."

"He died a few days after we arrived. A freak accident: hit by a runaway carriage as he crossed the street." Robert's voice carried a suspicious monotone?as if denying the death of his friend had any impact on him.

"I'm so sorry," Johanna squeezed his hand, leaning closer. "And that's why you're always in black." She couldn't imagine life without Ava. They'd been friends for so long; it would be like losing a part of her. "How long had you known each other?"

"Twelve years...We met in the war." Robert pulled his hand back and abruptly stood, shaking out his coat. "Enough talking; we have patients to see." And off he went down the sidewalk, leaving her to scramble to catch up and dodge other pedestrians. She shouldn't have expected anything different. Every time they veered close to an intimate topic, he shut down, running away.

"Slow down!" She called in an unladylike shout. Several ladies glared at her and tipped up their noses at such behavior, but she didn't care. Lifting her burgundy skirts, she tried to avoid the maze of puddles. "Dr. Forrester!" The firmer tone seemed to get his attention as he slowed enough for her to catch up.

Splashes of water wet his pant legs after sloshing through puddles left by early showers. The fresh scent of rain had washed away the stench of garbage as they'd traipsed through the close-quartered streets.

"If you can't keep up, perhaps you're not cut out for this particular job."

"*Perhaps* I could keep up, if I grew six inches, or someone learned to walk at a respectable pace instead of galloping off when the conversation became uncomfortable."

"And maybe someone should learn boundaries," he said as they arrived at their next patient's home. They stood on opposite sides of the doorway, arms crossed in front of their chests, challenging the other's claim.

Johanna respected boundaries, but at this point, it seemed like Robert had formed a small cage around him meant to keep *everyone* out. And she was determined to release him.

Chapter Fourteen

"How long did it take for Mrs. Potts to open up to you?" Johanna asked a few days later, frustration lacing her voice. They'd finished a patient visit down in the hotel kitchens where she'd pushed and prodded to no avail. Mrs. Potts remained stubbornly tight-lipped when it came to Johanna's pressing.

"Perhaps if you listened more than you talked, you'd get somewhere," he suggested. Paintings of peaceful landscapes lined the hall as they walked back to his office. Several parts of the hotel housed various themes when it came to decor. They were currently near the healing waters of Bath or the rolling green of the Highlands depending which way one looked.

"Hard to listen when no one's saying anything."

"Hard to say anything when someone's talking your ear off," Robert retorted. While he enjoyed learning more about her through the stories she shared, it wasn't conducive to getting his patients to open up. Most of them had never experienced a ball or even been to the country; they couldn't relate to Johanna's rambling anecdotes.

"It's a nervous habit." The mumbled words tugged at him; he didn't like the dejected note he heard.

Sighing, he pulled her to a stop. Squeezing her arm, he said, "Look, Mrs. Potts, Mr. Hobbs, all of our patients, they're not used to a lady like you in their space, let alone wanting to know about their lives. If you give them time and opportunity," he emphasized that last bit with a meaningful look, "then they may be more amenable to conversation."

Light brown eyes stared up at him in contemplation, and he found himself mesmerized by the flecks of gold he found. He didn't think he'd ever seen eyes that color before. "You may have a point...I suppose I'm not used to being expected to re-main silent." She shrugged beneath his touch.

"Really?" He figured her husband would've preferred her to stay quiet like most men of the nobility: their wives were meant for decoration not conversation.

"I told you, I have a way of connecting with people. Obvi-ously, it doesn't work on everyone, but when Howard hosted parties, he expected me to keep everyone happy. I guess I never dropped the habit of always having to be 'on', so to speak. I'll try to tone it down." She stepped back and then continued for-ward as he followed behind. He hadn't expected such an in-sight into her past life, but it explained a lot. Looking back, he realized Johanna always kept the conversation going, even when he'd prefer she didn't. It must be exhausting.

When he caught up to her, she tilted her head up as a pleased smile tugged at her lips, surprising him with the change of mood. "You said 'our patients' back there. I'm glad you agree."

A rueful chuckle vibrated through him. "Slip of the tongue, nothing more."

She hummed in disbelief, "Keep thinking that." And they fell into playful banter as they continued their rounds for the day.

After their last patient, Robert was locking up the office when a young boy ran up to them with wild hair and his arms waving frantically. "Please, sir, you must come quick!"

"What is it, lad?" Robert lowered to his haunches to meet the boy eye to eye. He could tell the little ragamuffin hadn't bathed in a while as dirt concealed most of his face.

"My brother, he's been hurt! Doc Lane's gone to see to Mrs. Humphrey's baby, and we need someone now!" The boy's exclamations became louder and more agitated as he pulled his worn cap down, wringing it between his hands.

"Don't worry; we'll help you. Just show us the way," Robert said. Whipping around the boy raced ahead of them as they followed. He led them back to the rookery, into a building so dilapidated he could scarcely believe someone could live inside. Johanna must've agreed since a quiet sound of distress left her as they entered. Wooden boards meant to cover the window lay swaying in a slight breeze and provided no protection from the elements.

As they walked deeper into the dark home, they could hear a man cursing loudly in the back. He watched a flush creep up Johanna's neck at the colorful language. By now, he figured it was something she'd become accustomed to, but apparently not.

"Pete, it's about fucking time! Who've you brought with you? Because I'm liable to cut this damned leg off myself!" A younger man with shaggy blonde hair lay in bed hunched over his stretched-out leg; Robert could see blood staining the rags he held to it. A wooden log sat on the ground beside him.

"That won't be necessary. I'm Dr. Robert Forrester, and this is my assistant, Mrs. Johanna Milton. What's your name and what happened?" He knelt before the man and began peeling back the layers of soaked cloth. Johanna's nose wrinkled at the smell of iron permeating the air. This wasn't the first time they'd dealt with a bleeding wound, but this one looked particularly gruesome.

"Jonathan Travers. A damn beam fell on me while I was sleeping." No wonder, he thought, as he glanced upwards and saw the tattered remains of a floor above. It looked like a demolition zone here; he didn't understand what would drive the man to live in such a place.

"Sleeping during the day?"

"I keep odd hours," Travers said behind gritted teeth as Robert probed the wound causing a fresh spurt of blood.

"I see; well, I'll have to clean this which will hurt like the devil. Then I'll stitch it up which will be even worse. Do you have any brandy or whiskey available? It might help dull your senses."

"Pete, you know where to look." The boy took off and returned with half a bottle of Jameson. Travers took a large gulp before motioning for Robert to continue. "Get on with it, then. I'll just be drinking my pain away as I enjoy the sight of the beautiful Mrs. Milton."

Robert stopped what he was doing to glance up at her. "Yes, she *is* beautiful...Now, hang on, and we'll set you to rights soon enough." He didn't know what had possessed him to say such a thing, but her shy smile was worth it.

Focus. Turning back to the injury, he doused it with a solution of saltwater which sent Travers into another round of expletives. Biting back his amusement at some of the interesting pairings, he beckoned Johanna closer. "I need you to hold the wound closed as I sew him up; make sure the skin's aligned correctly."

She balked at the direction, tossing a look of fear at the ragged edges he was talking about. "I don't feel qualified to do that."

"Oh, I'm sorry. Have you suddenly come to your senses without my knowledge? No? Then do as I asked." Amusement filled him over her hesitancy; this was exactly what she signed up for, after all, even if this was the worst injury she'd seen.

"You have a wicked sense of humor, sir," she said, relenting and moving to do as he demanded.

He threaded the sewing needle, muttering, "And to think, that's not even the most wicked thing about me." A scarlet blush bloomed on her cheeks as she caught the quiet words, but this was no time for more teasing. He waited for her to settle before stitching the torn skin and rebandaging it with clean cloths, replacing the dirty rags he'd initially found.

"That should do for now. You'll need to stay off the leg for about a week as it heals; you don't want to risk it reopening and getting infected. As is, you're still at risk of an infection."

"Thanks, doc. And you, too, love." It was clear the whiskey Travers had downed was starting to take effect as he winked at Johanna, and Robert resisted the warning growl building in his chest. *Time to go.*

Turning to the boy, Pete, he repeated himself to make sure someone took proper care of the wound. "Remember: keep it as clean as you can, and we'll be back to check on it next week."

"Good day, Mr. Travers. Please heed Dr. Forrester's instructions," Johanna said, then they left the man and boy and headed home.

"Well, he's certainly an interesting man."

"Mmm...most likely a criminal," he said darkly.

"What makes you say that?" Her brows knitted at the accusation, but he didn't think he was wrong.

"Why else would he hide out in a ruin such as that unless he was hiding from the police?" Any reasonable person would choose a home that wasn't falling around them, endangering them even as they slept, even the residents of Devil's Haven. Yet, Travers bucked the usual sense of self-preservation.

"You may have a point." She bit her lip as she contemplated the idea, though it didn't put her off his case. "Nevertheless, we'll still care for him; it doesn't really matter if he's a criminal or not."

No, it didn't, but he was impressed that she was okay with the notion. Most of polite society turned up their noses at such men; yet here again, Johanna flouted Society's rules and chose to follow her own path.

Wonders never cease to amaze.

"SO, WHAT'S GOING ON between you and Mrs. Milton?" Porter raised his wrapped hands in defense before Robert could respond. It was the day after their rush to Travers' aid, and Porter had dragged him to his club in another offer of friendship. "And don't say you're just working together. It's been weeks now that the two of you have spent every day in close confines. And I've seen the way you look at her."

Robert was still unsure about that prediction, but he had to concede that he enjoyed the physical activity. He didn't know why he hadn't considered joining such an establishment before, since exercise tended to help his state of mind. They circled each other in the ring, the sweat dripping down their bare chests a testament to how long they've sparred.

"I don't look at her any particular way," he said, unwilling to admit to the desire he felt in her presence. Porter was enough of a busybody, if Robert told him about wanting Johanna, he'd never hear the end of it.

"Right. And I'm the King of England," Porter said as he blocked a punch. They were well-matched, both of similar size. Other groups of men surrounded them as they worked on rowing machines, club swinging, or one of the other machines available.

"Jo...," Robert corrected himself, "Mrs. Milton is attractive; I won't deny it. But that doesn't mean there's anything untoward going on. She assists me; we have a professional relationship." After she decided to take his advice and listen more, the people they saw started responding to her questions more. It surprised him to learn so much about his patients.

But Johanna had a way about her.

"Of course," Porter said, "How are your patients? Mrs. Wyland approached me before she departed, expressing her gratitude again for your assistance after her incident." Robert threw a left jab and caught Porter in the ribs. Doubled over in pain, he let out a curse.

Robert waited for Porter to gather himself, resting his fists on his hips. "I should thank her. If her corset hadn't been too tight, I wouldn't have met Mrs. Milton."

"And what a tragedy that would've been."

Robert silently agreed. They spent the next few hours talking about their work and sparring. The camaraderie felt good, though uneasy at times, when he recalled past chats with Harry.

Maybe Porter was right, and it was time for him to open up to someone. He wasn't ready to share about his attacks, but perhaps a bit of his life wouldn't be so bad.

Chapter Fifteen

"Out spake their Captain brave and bold:
A merry wight was he:
Though London Tower were Michael's hold,
We'll set Trelawny free!"

THE SLURRED LYRICS hit Robert like a cannonball to the chest. A group of drunk soldiers hung on to each other as they stumbled through the lobby, one by one trying to outdo the other by increasing the volume and fervor of their song. As if physically struck, he brought a hand to his heart to rub away the stinging sensation.

The folk ditty was a common tune heard around military camps, the jaunty melody raising the men's spirits. Robert remembered a time spent around a blazing fire; they sang and drank from tin cups filled with watered-down ale.

"Honestly, isn't it a bit early for them to be so inebriated?" Johanna sniffed in disgust as the young men made fools of themselves. He noticed a few hotel workers approach, trying to usher them into a more private space. No doubt drunken men were a bad look for the St. James.

"They recently returned from the Magdala; I suppose they believe they've earned the right to drink whenever and however much they want." Porter had informed him of the envoy's previous location as he lamented the length of their stay. Their raucous presence in the hotel irritated some of the patrons, and Robert couldn't say he disagreed.

"Wasn't there a fight there or something?"

"A battle," he supplied. "We won."

They followed the movements of the group as they disappeared from the lobby, their loud voices muffled the further they went.

"What a relief!" Johanna said before changing subjects. "Would you care to join me for dinner?"

The abrupt switch and request caught him off guard. Women didn't invite men to their private suites, no matter how innocuous 'dinner' might be.

"I don't think that would be appropriate; I'm surprised I have to lecture you on the impropriety," he answered, the need to get away urging him forward. His skin pulsated with a tingling sensation, electricity running through his veins as his heart rate sped up. The soldiers' song replayed through his mind on a never-ending loop.

Weaving between milling guests, he tried to escape Johanna in the crowd. One would think he'd realize it's impossible to lose her by this point. When she wanted something, she didn't give up easily.

"It's not as if we have matchmaking mamas staring over our shoulders," she huffed as she took the stairs two at a time to keep up with him. "We're two grown adults who can handle eating a meal together. Besides, the horse is out of the barn already. Or have you forgotten our kisses?"

At the top of the steps, his eyes traveled from her heaving form to the wall behind them, the memory of the last time they stood in this spot coming back to haunt him. No, he hadn't forgotten about those. But even recalling their past indiscretions couldn't tamp down his overstimulated body. He needed time away from her—from everyone—to calm down.

He forced himself to grit out, "It doesn't matter. I'm not interested." Flashes of heat caused sweat to form on his body only for a chill to freeze him as it cooled. *Ninety-nine, ninety-eight, ninety-seven.*

"You have to eat, don't you? Why can't you dine with me?" Johanna tried a different tack and followed him to his suite's door. Relief at being so close to sanctuary barely banked the attack taking its toll on him.

"Because I don't want to."

"That...Are you alright?" Her concerned eyes took in the sweat on his brow and his flushed skin.

"I'd be better if you weren't badgering me about this damned dinner." Pulling out his key, he attempted to insert it into the door lock, but his shaking hand kept missing the opening.

"I don't think this is about a meal..." Johanna watched as he tried again. "Was it the soldiers again? You've been avoiding the topic for weeks now. Perhaps in a more private setting, you'd be willing to share; obviously, there's something you need to work out. And I'm happy to lend a listening ear."

He jerked at the question. If only the stubborn key would go where it was supposed to. "This isn't some Sunday gossip between ladies," he said. "You don't know what you're asking...Goddamit, why won't this go into the damned lock?"

"Here, let me." She cupped his tight fist, prying the frustrating metal from his hand, "I'm not some frail matron; I can handle whatever you have to say. And while I enjoy discussing fashion and charities, I'm not so shallow that I can't have a serious conversation. You should know that by now," she scolded. Too easily, she slipped the key in the latch and a click sounded as the mechanism unlocked.

He shook his head in disgust, "You want to know some deep dark secret, thinking you can fix me. But it doesn't work that way; what do you know about pain and trauma? You're a lady raised in Society—the most traumatic experience you've probably had was finding a husband, and you managed to find one after all."

"You know nothing of my life before coming here; pain is not exclusive to you." Her mouth clenched in a grim line. For a moment, he wondered about her past and the sadness he saw in her eyes before his problems pushed to the forefront again.

Heavy breaths fell from him, his heart threatening to beat out of his chest. "Do you ever stop with the interrogations? Leave it alone." He jerked the key out of the lock, opened the door, and turned to shut it in her face.

"I'm just trying to help; why is that so hard for you?"

"I don't need your help; I never asked for it. And while we're on the subject: your constant questioning does the exact opposite of helping me. Now, good night." He slammed the door on her shocked form, ready to end their conversation. He expected her to pound on the door until he relented but blessed quiet greeted him. Stripping down, he resumed his usual position on the floor: counting out the exercises as he focused on the childhood memory with his mother.

A trickle of fear penetrated him, a worry that he'd never be free of this torturous process.

Chapter Sixteen

Johanna limited her words the next few days. Robert's comment about badgering him with questions stuck with her and reminded her of the issues she had connecting with patients before she took his advice. It seemed that none of her old tactics for conversation worked when it came to the Manchester community.

Sighing, she tried to focus on Bessie's story about her son as Robert rewrapped her gout-ridden foot. He could be so gentle, careful to apply just the right pressure, and always sure to comfort the patient with a calm voice. The change in his demeanor shocked her each time, as it was such a marked difference from how he treated everyone outside a patient's home.

"And that's when my Matthew decided to leave and make his fortune elsewhere," Bessie finished with a wistful sigh and took another bite of the sheep trotter Johanna had brought.

"Thank you for sharing Bessie; he sounds like a lovely man," she fibbed, but there was no need to upset the woman by insulting her errant son. Taking the scissors and surgical tape from Robert once he'd finished, she packed them away in his leather bag before rising to her feet in the crowded room.

In the beginning, she'd asked if Bessie would like help tidying up, but the woman had refused. Now Johanna kept quiet about the state of the small home, ignoring the stench of mold that clung to the faded walls.

"We're finished, Bessie. Try to keep that clean, okay?" Robert gestured to the bandaged foot. Once they said their goodbyes and stepped outside, Johanna held out her hands for the small bowl he pulled out of his bag. After each patient, he washed his hands. Unscrewing the top of a canister holding water, he poured some in the bowl before scrubbing down with a bar of soap. She noticed his hands looked better; he must be using the hand cream she gave him for dryness.

"Are you going to give me the silent treatment from now on?" He asked, his eyes focused on what he was doing. The question surprised her. She thought he'd be grateful for the quiet; it'd been his number one request for weeks now.

"I'm trying to listen to your advice. Not be so chatty," she said, dumping the water in the alley once he was done. He handed her a washcloth, so she could dry the tin bowl before placing it back in his bag.

"While I'm impressed with your commitment, I don't expect you to not speak at all." He avoided eye contact as he continued. "And I apologize for my attitude the other night. It...wasn't a good time."

She refrained from commenting on that last statement, though curiosity scratched at her. She was desperate to know about his past and why he reacted so strongly to the military regiment.

"Thank you for the apology, and I'm sorry for making you feel as if you were withstanding an inquisition."

They stood awkwardly, facing each other, and looking anywhere but at the other. Johanna had never had this type of conversation with Howard; he'd never apologized for anything. It was a new experience.

Breaking the silence, Robert asked, "How'd you get Chef Le Beau to make sheep trotter? I would've thought he'd turn his nose up at such a humble dish."

"One word: persistence."

There was a pause as Robert's mouth twitched, and she struggled to keep her own composure. But the battle was lost when he broke down in laughter. They must've looked a sight, standing in the middle of Devil's Haven giggling like a couple of schoolchildren, but it felt good to finally release the tension that had built between them.

"Why doesn't that surprise me? Le Beau didn't stand a chance."

"I'll admit, he resisted longer than I thought he would — especially since I'm a guest of the hotel. You'd think I could get whatever I want; no questions asked." She shrugged in bewilderment, but let it go. In the end, she got what she wanted, and Bessie had enjoyed her favorite meal which was all that really mattered.

"Well, we should get going," Robert said after they'd settled down, "Mr. Travers will be expecting us." Following beside him as he headed towards Travers's home, she mulled over broaching the topic of dinner again now that they'd made up. Deciding to go for it, she asked, "Would you join me for supper tomorrow night?"

Robert's brows furrowed as he glanced over at her, "I thought we covered this already."

"That was before we came to an understanding. I promise I won't hound you with questions. We can talk about anything."

Or do anything, she thought with a blush. It had been a while since their last kiss, and she was eager to continue their passionate exploration.

"And, of course, you care nothing for propriety," he sighed, dodging a pack of running children. Their laughs echoed through the street causing a sharp pain to prick her heart.

"I think that proverbial ship sailed once I started accompanying you on house calls."

When Mr. Travers's rundown building came into view, Robert stopped, rubbing a hand down his cheek. "You have a point...I suppose dinner wouldn't be so bad. As long as you guarantee: no interrogations." A firm glare met her hopeful gaze. Bouncing on her heels in excitement, she crossed a finger over her heart.

"I promise! I'll expect you at seven o'clock sharp, and if you don't show up, I *will* come and get you." She let the threat fall between them as her eyes narrowed, daring him to doubt her. Nodding acquiescence, he knocked on the front door of their next appointment, and she released a breath of relief.

Pete, the young boy from before, opened the door before ushering them in. This was a courtesy call to check on Travers after their last emergency visit, and Johanna prayed he was healing well after his ordeal. The man still had a lot of life ahead of him; it would be a shame for it to be cut short because of an accident.

"Ah, the good doctor has returned, and he brought his pretty assistant," Travers said. He lay propped up against a few worn pillows on a small bed set against the window. Not that it did much good with so much grime blocking most of the light.

"I see you're in much better spirits. Can I assume your leg is healing well?" Robert set his bag down on a dusty side table and began pulling out his stethoscope. She moved closer and continued setting up the rest of his supplies.

"It still hurts like hell, but I'm managing it. It helps that you've brought along such a lovely distraction," Travers tossed a lopsided smile in her direction. "How are you today, Mrs. Milton? Is doc treating you alright?"

"He's treating me perfectly well, thank you." She continued her tasks and wondered that she didn't blush at his flirting. Was she so enamored with Robert that she couldn't even respond to another man anymore? That didn't bode well for her future.

"Well, damn. I thought I might steal you away; sometimes I wonder if I couldn't use a bit of a feminine touch, if you know what I mean."

"That's enough," Robert said, low and angry. "Mrs. Milton is a lady. Behave yourself, or you can see to your own injuries." He stepped back as if threatening his departure, but Travers held his hands up in supplication.

"Relax; I'm only teasing, Mrs. Milton, right?"

Johanna met Robert's stormy gaze and gave a signal that she was fine. "Of course, Mr. Travers. No harm done; now let's see to that leg."

Much of the next half hour passed with Robert performing his usual examination, cleaning Travers' wound, then rewrapping it. Once he'd dispensed with his usual list of instructions for care, they left and headed home, finally finished for the day.

"He's a bit of a scoundrel, isn't he?" she asked as they passed through the hotel doors. Decorated by stained glass florals, it was one of the many beautiful touches Mr. Porter had commissioned for the building.

"That's one word for him," Robert grumbled. A brief chuckle bubbled up at his surliness; it was sweet how upset he'd gotten over Travers' remarks. Could he be jealous?

Deciding to test her theory, she said, "You're right: charming and handsome would also work well."

"I know what you're doing." He didn't spare her a glance as they kept walking up the staircase to their respective rooms. "And it won't end well for you."

Hmm...that sounds promising.

"I'm not sure what you mean, sir. I was just enumerating a few of Mr. Travers's assets."

"And trying to rile me up in the process, I wager." Yes, she did like the direction this was taking.

Deciding to up the ante, she tapped a finger against her chin as if considering a new idea. "He does seem quite taken with me. Perhaps I'll stop by with something from the kitchens. Do you think he'd prefer strawberry or?"

Spying an open closet filled with cleaning supplies, Robert pulled her behind him and slammed the door shut. "You will not bring him desserts. You will not visit him alone; I forbid it." The doorknob dug into her back as he pressed closer to her, but she didn't care. A rush of excitement coursed through her at their proximity in this private oasis.

"You can't be serious."

"As a heart attack."

"That's terrible," she said as she punched his shoulder but couldn't resist a short laugh.

He shrugged. "Just a little doctor humor...But we're getting off course. You're not to see Travers alone, understand?"

Just like that, heat flooded her and shot her reckless yearnings to the forefront. It had been weeks since their last kiss, and she wanted the streak to end today. Now.

Forgetting about pushing him further, she took the reins in her own hands and lifted up until her mouth brushed against his. He stilled, his hands hovering at his sides, before yanking her into his firm body. Immediately, she softened and wrapped her arms around his neck.

His tongue dueled with her own as she matched his fervor. Kissing Robert never grew old, with each time more heated and frantic than the last. She supposed she should feel shame at initiating such contact, but none could be found. Instead, all she felt was joy and pleasure.

A sigh escaped her as he pulled back; she wasn't ready for this to end. Sucking on his bottom lip, she pulled him deeper into her even as his hoarse, "Johanna," echoed in the small space. His hands roamed lower to cup her bottom, hoisting her up until her burning center met his arousal. Moaning, she rubbed against him like a cat in heat, anxious for more.

"Johanna...Jo...we have to stop. Anyone could find us here," he whispered despite his continued rocking against her core.

"Don't care," she mumbled, moving to kiss his cheek and neck. Stubble scratched her, so different from her own smooth skin. A breathless laugh reached her ears as he gently detangled her from him.

"I do. I don't want us forced to do something we'll regret." He meant marriage. That cast a pall over her desire.

Letting him separate them, she watched as he ran a hand through his mussed hair and adjusted himself, the act sending a flare of need through her. No, she didn't want to trap him; she wasn't even sure she wanted to remarry, though children were something she'd always wanted.

She rubbed her suddenly weary eyes at how complicated things were becoming, yet she couldn't stop this train even if she wanted to. Whatever was happening between them would need to be seen through to the end, one way or another.

"You're right; we don't want to be caught," she said. "I'll leave now, and you can follow a few minutes after...But I will still see you tomorrow for our dinner?" Perhaps it was unwise to continue down this dangerous path, but no matter her concerns, the fact remained that she wanted him. Wanted him with a desperation she'd never known before.

He sighed, quiet for a moment, before accepting her invitation. "Yes, you'll see me tomorrow."

Releasing her breath, she touched a hand to his cheek before peeking out the door to see it was clear and returning to her room.

Tomorrow.

Chapter Seventeen

Johanna ordered a special dinner to be set before her guest arrived and warned her lady's maid that she wouldn't be needed for the evening. Tonight, would be spent learning more about Robert, without overstepping his boundaries, of course, and continuing their flirtation. Though, flirtation might be too tame a word at this point; they'd progressed well past that the night before. She amazed herself with her boldness but liked this newfound confidence she had to take charge of her life.

Going for what she wanted had gotten her a position as Robert's assistant, perhaps she'd strike gold the second time as well.

After changing into a silk evening gown that revealed much more skin than her serviceable daily dresses, she made sure everything was ready for Robert's arrival before waiting impatiently in the greeting room.

If Ava knew what she was up to...A grin crept over her face as she imagined her friend's shock and awe. Johanna may have always been an outgoing social butterfly, but she'd always kept within Society's rules. Now, she was breaking free.

A short knock on the door caused her to jump in her seat. Placing a hand over her racing heart, she forced herself to walk normally to the door instead of rushing over and throwing it open. Nerves and excitement mingled in her blood, making her feel a little dizzy; she needed to calm down. He was just a man. A man she was intensely curious about and attracted to, but a man, nonetheless.

Taking a deep breath and releasing it, she opened the door and observed he'd taken the time to change and clean up. His jaw looked freshly-shaven, clear of any scruff from earlier, and his short hair gleamed with drops of water.

"I'm here," he said, his lack of excitement a direct contrast to her buoyant nature. On the surface, they seemed so different, but she'd seen him with patients—with them he showed a lighter, friendlier side. She just needed to reach that part of him, prove that she could be trusted with such vulnerability.

"I can see that; please come in." She stood to the side and motioned him forward. Cautious steps brought him to the center of the room, his hands remaining stuffed in his pockets as she felt a wave of protectiveness come over her at the sight of his awkward uncertainty.

"Follow me; dinner is set up back here." She led him through a short hallway, bypassing the small water closet, to the dining room. Mr. Porter had outdone himself when he'd built this behemoth of a hotel. Each suite modeled a London flat; one could forget they weren't staying in a private residence.

The dinner table lay before them covered in all sorts of dishes. On closer inspection, she realized she may have been too enthusiastic considering it would only be the two of them, but she didn't know what Robert liked and wanted to be sure there'd be something to entice him. Besides her, of course.

"Are you expecting anyone else?" He eyed the massive amount of food warily. A tureen of crayfish soup sat near the center of the table while salmon with Dutch sauce and black game lay on either side of it. Various sides of potatoes and French beans mingled with the numerous appetizers. Then there was the compote of fruit and raspberry tart for dessert.

"It's just the two of us. I mentioned to Emma that I'd have a guest for dinner, so she could notify the kitchen. They might have gone a tad overboard." *More than a tad.* The meal was beginning to overwhelm *her* the longer she stared at it. Making a broad gesture to encompass the full table before them, she tried to move them back on course. "We'll do what we can; please sit."

"I may not be a gentleman, but I know the lady is supposed to be seated first." Robert pulled out the velvet-covered chair at the head of the table before taking the seat next to her. Candlelight played over his masculine features, highlighting his sharp jaw.

After an awkward pause, they began eating and sticking to safe topics. When a lull occurred towards the end, Johanna seized the opportunity to press deeper. Wanting to know more about him, she decided to risk upsetting him with the question at the forefront of her mind. And if he didn't answer then she'd give up as she'd promised.

"So, we've had a couple of run-ins with the soldiers staying here lately, and each time you react negatively...Why?" She decided to get straight to the point since he was a no-nonsense type of person. He coughed as the drink he took went down the wrong way.

Grabbing a napkin and wiping his mouth, he turned to her, "You don't pull your punches, do you?"

Shrugging, she said, "I know it's not your favorite subject, but I had to try one last time."

The table rattled as his knee bounced erratically underneath, bumping the wooden top. He dropped a hand to steady it before reaching for the tart only to divert to a bread roll and begin tearing it into tiny, agitated pieces. "I told you I was in the war; I was an army surgeon like Harry. When I see those soldiers..." He tossed the demolished roll to his plate before sinking back into his chair. "They remind me of that time which you can imagine isn't pleasant."

"I?"

"And that's all I'll say about it." He cut her off. Closing her mouth, she shot him a rueful grin, but at least he'd given her some kind of insight into his past.

It occurred to her, like a fog being driven away by the sun, giving her acute clarity, that in all her questions, she'd failed to reciprocate that what she asked of him. Perhaps she needed to be more forthcoming with her own life if she were to ever have a hope of being let into his.

Taking a deep breath, she sat back and stared at the lace tablecloth in front of her, toying with the delicate edge. "Thank you for sharing with me...I suppose it's only fair if I reciprocate." She looked up with a brief smile that more resembled a grimace. "My marriage wasn't a happy one." Robert paused his nervous fidgeting to glance at her. "During my Seasons, my penchant for conversation and lack of a dowry put off potential suitors. I tried to temper myself, but it was difficult to listen to someone go on about something without interjecting a question or two."

"Naturally," he agreed, a wry smile brightening his face. She returned it briefly; he knew all too well her love of chatting.

"So, at the end of my second Season, with no betrothal in sight, my uncle introduced my father to a friend of his, Sir Howard Milton, another lowly baron who had made some sound investments and was willing to pay a hefty price for a child-bearing bride. I know it's unusual; it's customary for the bride's family to offer a dowry instead of the other way around. But my father had gambling debts that had eaten away the dowry I did have. Howard was willing to pay those off. You see, his first marriage had ended prematurely when his wife died of pneumonia, leaving no children behind."

"So, a deal was struck," Robert filled in as she paused, remembering that fateful day when her father had notified her of her impending nuptials. What a terrible day it had been, learning she would be married to a man almost three times her age.

"At first, Howard was cordial; he was desperate for an heir. But as time passed and I failed to conceive, he became...less so. He turned to other women, searching for the woman who could give him a child, all the while expecting me to make the most of my only 'useful' skill?talking. He figured I could at least keep his guests happy and open to his business advances. There was always some sort of transaction occurring at our parties." She paused as she remembered those days, a far-off look entering her eyes. "'Put on a smile, gel', he'd say...It's funny how such a command can elicit the opposite reaction." The edge of the tablecloth lay frayed now, loose threads drifting over her lap.

He reached over to calm her picking, bringing her hand to rest on the table. "What happened to him?"

"Stroke from old age at seventy-one; a decade of marriage finally over. That was two years ago."

Robert made a hum of understanding, the tips of his fingers stroking the back of her hand in a soothing gesture. "Ah, you've just come out of mourning then, haven't you?"

"Yes, and when my friend, Ava, invited me to Manchester I jumped at the chance for a change of scenery. And pace, to be honest. When I arrived, I felt energized and free to do whatever I wanted."

"Which is why you were so stubborn about helping me," Robert squeezed her hand. "Now things are starting to make sense, although I still don't understand why you'd choose to work."

"My brother-in-law is the heir now. He wrote me a letter not long after I got here basically wishing me the best but not to come back. The stipend he offered wouldn't even cover my stay here, so it became a bit of a necessity." Humiliation pricked her skin at the confession. She'd been brought so low that day, but, thankfully, God had smiled down on her and turned her situation around.

"What a cad! What self-respecting man leaves his family practically destitute?" Robert squeezed her hand harder as his righteous anger for her rose. She appreciated his defense, especially since no one had ever cared enough to do such a thing.

"Well, we were never close..."

"Nonsense; you're his sister-in-law. You spent holidays and birthdays together for ten years, and this is how he treats you? I've a mind to ride out to whatever backwater he's in and give him a piece of my mind."

"Thank you, but that won't be necessary. I appreciate..." A choking hiccup cut her off, her throat constricting as a well of emotions rushed forth. Here was a man who'd known her for only a few months, and he could see the problems with Richard's decision, yet Richard had known her for a decade and could kick her out to the streets and still sleep at night. They were like night and day. An unsurprising realization as Richard resembled Howard, and she'd already discovered how much he'd been lacking compared to Robert.

Their eyes connected for a long moment, an unspoken bond forming, before the intensity became too much and they looked away. "Well," she released a nervous laugh and dabbed at her eyes. "I asked you to dinner to learn more about you, and here I am spilling my sordid past, not what I had planned." She brushed a strand of hair off her face, rising out of her seat so they could retire to the parlor.

Following her steps, Robert said, "No, but I appreciate your candor; it helps me understand you better." He moved behind her, his hands resting on the exposed skin of her shoulders. The sudden touch made her twitch as the mood shifted. Leaning in so his mouth hovered above her ear, he added, "And demands that I try to help you forget such bad treatment."

The brush of his lips whisked over her neck down to the crook of her shoulder where he gave a teasing nip; it conjured the memory of their interlude in the alley—except this time fabric didn't separate his gentle bite from her skin.

A shiver of awareness settled in her stomach. She wondered how far he would go, now that they didn't have the possibility of witnesses to their impropriety. It seemed this part of her plan would be coming true, she thought happily, as his hands caressed her bare arms before curling around her waist. She'd forgone a corset, imagining exactly this: giving him easy access to her body.

Noticing the softness beneath his hand instead of firm boning, he dragged her closer to him, his arousal digging into her backside. "No corset?" His lips moved to kiss the top of her shoulder.

Tilting her head to the side, she rested against him. "I didn't think it was necessary."

His hum of approval vibrated through her as he murmured, "Good girl," before unlacing her gown. Blue ribbon fluttered down her chest as the front began to gape open, revealing the thin white chemise underneath. His warm hand drifted inside to cup one of her breasts and lifted the globe as he circled the sensitive tip.

"I won't take you tonight," he said. "But I can please you in other ways..."

A stab of disappointment shot through her at his statement, though she knew logically it was too soon to progress straight to the bedroom. Such an intimate act required a level of trust they hadn't achieved yet. But at least he was willing to give her a small taste of what she'd missed with Howard, and that would be enough for now.

"Should we move to the chaise?" she suggested, impressed with the daring question. Perhaps she could hold her own in these passion plays, despite her lack of experience in seduction.

"So eager?" He asked as he withdrew his hand and led her to the sturdy lounger dominating the room. A few steps forward, though, sent Johanna tripping over the sagging hem of her gown. She catapulted into his back before righting herself.

An embarrassed laugh escaped, red blooming on her cheeks, "I guess I need a little more practice in these affairs...Step one: remember to lift your undone dress or else risk falling flat on your face." Fearing she ruined the mood, she watched carefully as Robert took in her bedraggled state. Slowly, a grin appeared, revealing an amused smile.

"You do keep things interesting, don't you, Jo?" A low chuckle rumbled through him, and she allowed herself to breathe a sigh of relief. Sexual relations were always shrouded in solemnity; they were meant for procreation—which was a very serious task, according to her mother, who'd explained everything right before her wedding ceremony. And while she assumed there was an element of pleasure to be had, she hadn't realized it could also include laughter. The things she was learning, and he'd barely touched her!

"It seems I can't help myself." She shrugged and one of her sleeves drooped lower. His gaze immediately darted to the action, heat reigniting in the dark irises.

"Let me take care of getting you safely to your destination." With that declaration, he scooped her up and carried her to the settee where he eased her down with tenderness. Taking a step back, he studied her form before commanding her to lift her dress. "Pull it up, so I can see your lovely thighs, sweetheart."

Tucking her knees together, she reached down to scrunch the silky fabric into a wrinkled mess on her lap. Cool air passed over the heated skin left open to his attention. Her silk stockings provided no protection as they reached to her thighs and met garters showcasing little blue rosebuds.

"Beautiful..." he murmured. Returning to her, he lowered both arms behind her head to rest on the curved back of the lounger, caging her underneath him. His heavy breaths filled the room and his nose flared as he inhaled her scent.

Bending lower, he brought his lips to hers. The soft touch contrasted with their previous encounters of rough and tumble passion. This spoke of a tenderness that melted any resistance she may have had. Only their mouths touched, all sensation radiating from this small electrifying spot. Time slowed as if they were moving through molasses, each unhurried stroke of the tongue like drawing honey from a comb.

She never wanted it to end, but of course, as the thought occurred, Robert pulled away as he made his way lower. Sinking to his knees in front of her, he tugged the thin chemise tight against her skin, so her hardened nipples stood in stark relief. His prize exposed, he sucked one sensitive tip into wet heat as she pressed closer, a short gasp falling from her. Satisfied with his handiwork, he switched sides until she was panting with need, her arousal coming to a sharp peak between her thighs.

Lowering still, he urged, "Place your leg over the arm like this." He raised the exposed limb until it hooked over the edge of the chair in an indecent pose that widened her to his gaze. A soft whimper left her at the exposure, uncomfortable with such vulnerability.

"Robert..." she began to protest, but he swept a soothing caress over her worried face.

"Relax, sweetheart. Don't be afraid..." he said as he bent to kiss the inside of her knee, his dark eyes holding hers. She wasn't sure about this new direction as he kissed a path up the delicate skin of her thigh until he reached the apex.

This didn't seem like the usual way things were done. Although to be fair, Howard had never offered much more than a firm thrust of his member before finishing minutes later. She supposed that may have left her ignorant of certain lovemaking practices.

Robert's tongue licked up her center, shattering any thoughts she had of Howard. Her hips lifted off the chair at the contact, but his strong hands forced her back down. He spread her curls, eliciting another blush at the blatantly wet sound of her sex.

Robert seemed unbothered as he began licking and sucking her most intimate places. A rough groan of enjoyment met her ears as his tongue stroked her, wringing a gasp of pleasure from her. Soon he slid two fingers into her opening and slowly thrust inside, his mouth moving to the peak of her sex to nibble on the engorged bundle of nerves.

"Yes...please..." She arched up from the settee, reaching for some unknown plane, sparks of fire burning her skin as if she were hurtling towards the sun.

"Come for me, Jo...please, sweet girl, I need to hear you...need to feel..."

Her cry of release cut him off as the taut strand of tension snapped and her body experienced a cascade of ecstasy unlike anything she'd felt before. He guided her through her orgasm, prolonging the sensations as she clenched against his fingers. When at last, the intensity faded into a sated glow, he gave one last lick over her core before rising enough to kiss her. She tasted herself on his tongue, an unusual but not unpleasant flavor, her tired body responding to the sensual touch.

Her breathing evened as her eyes fluttered shut, exhaustion overcoming her. She felt Robert move away, and through her lashes, she saw him adjusting himself before retreating further.

"I must go now," he said, surprising her, splashing a bucket of water over the warm feeling of contentment she'd been bathing in.

"What? No...you..." She motioned vaguely to his obvious arousal, still unsatisfied.

"I'll be fine; I must leave now." He scrubbed his sleeve over the gleaming wetness that still shone from where his mouth had been only moments ago. Bewildered, Johanna dropped her leg to the carpet as she covered up.

"I don't understand; you don't have...I don't want you to go," she said, pushing the words past a lump in her throat.

Turning away, he muttered, "I have to go; this shouldn't have happened." Striding to the door without a backward glance, he left, the slam of the door echoing in the empty room.

Confusion washed over Johanna. Tingles of pleasure still shot off inside her like little fireworks, yet Robert had taken off like the hounds of hell were nipping at his heels. Did she do something wrong? He hadn't seemed displeased with her during their interlude, in fact, at times he'd seemed positively hungry for her.

But why disappear so quickly after such an earth-shattering moment? Disappointment curled through her as she wondered if perhaps it hadn't been so earth-shattering for him.

LATER THAT NIGHT, JOHANNA lay in bed twisting and turning, her head swirling with too many thoughts of earlier. Though she still felt upset over Robert's abrupt departure, righteous anger began brewing as she replayed the scene.

She'd let her walls down sharing about Howard and Richard, not to mention her physical vulnerability. She'd lain open to him, allowed his mouth to... A sound of frustration vibrated in her chest as unwanted curls of heat swirled through her at the memory. *Stop it!*

Switching sides, she punched her pillow as she tried to go to sleep. A small growl echoed in the room as the clock struck once signaling the early morning hour. Giving up, she made up her mind to get to the bottom of Robert's abrupt departure earlier. He would speak with her—tonight.

Jumping out of bed, she grabbed her wrapper and tied it over her nightgown. No need to dress this late in the evening; she doubted she'd run into many guests. Locking the door behind her, she marched down the hallway as they always remained well-lit for patrons.

Arriving at the end of the corridor in front of Robert's room, Johanna gave three loud knocks. Hopefully, his neighbors weren't light sleepers. She had no doubt, however, that *he* would still be awake. The dark circles ringing his eyes spoke of sleepless nights, another mark on her list of curiosities when it came to him. Her raised fist neared the door again before it was jerked open.

"What the hell are you thinking? It's the middle of the damn night!" His hair lay disheveled as he stood dressed in only a pair of hastily donned breeches—the buttons weren't even done up. Wide eyes traveled over his bare chest, following the enticing trail down to the open vee.

She'd yet to see so much of him, and it was quite a different view than she'd had of men before. At Howard's age, he'd been a jumble of wrinkly paper-thin skin topped by a round belly and balding head. Robert's virile body definitely did not fit that description.

"If you're finished...care to explain what you're doing here?" Amusement at her ogling almost overpowered his annoyance at the early morning wake up call. Her eyes snapped to his as she tried to convey a nonchalant attitude. Who cares if he's almost naked before her? *Not me.* No, she had more important tasks to see to.

Lifting her chin, she crossed her arms over her chest and said, "I've come to finish our conversation from earlier."

"As I recall, we did finish...or rather, *you* did." A cocky grin formed as he dared her to contradict the impertinent statement.

A red flush warmed her as arousal and frustration combined; he was being willfully ignorant.

"I'm talking about after...that happened...You just left without an explanation."

"You woke me up at one in the morning to pester me about that?"

"I wouldn't have to resort to drastic measures if you would just open up a little! I'm not asking for much, considering the intimate lengths we've gone so far!" Her raised voice brought a few pounding noises from some neighbors upset to be awakened at such an hour. She felt ridiculous shouting at him in her robe like a woman bound for Bedlam. Yet, his big body blocked entry into his suite. "Let me in," she demanded, sick of it, "This conversation needs to happen in private."

She waited for him to move, a long considering pause falling between them before he stepped aside. His lodgings matched hers in layout; the only difference being style. His tended towards more masculine decor with darker colors and leather furniture. She wondered if Mr. Porter purposely outfitted certain rooms for the sexes or if Robert had decorated himself.

Shaking her head at the stray thought, she refocused on getting answers from Robert.

Chapter Eighteen

"This conversation needs to not happen. Period," Robert retorted, annoyed yet impressed by her tenacity. "But since you're so hell-bent...Why not? It's not like I planned on sleeping much tonight anyway."

He dropped into a leather chair as she followed along and sat in its pair. They both sat facing the banked fire, only the flickering light from a candle brightening the dim room. He didn't know what to say, since he couldn't tell her the truth.

That he had to leave before the unfamiliar emotions ballooning inside led him to admit to feelings he couldn't have. That if he stayed a moment longer, he might've broken his promise not to take things any further. So, instead, he chose to throw her another bone and distract her by picking up their conversation from dinner. Somehow that now seemed to be the safer choice.

"I never planned on joining the military," he started, crossing a leg over one knee, his foot vibrating in agitation. "My father was the village doctor, and I wanted to take over his practice once he retired. Unfortunately, he died before I came of age." The dull ache of his death echoed beside the more intense pain of losing his mother and Harry. "I didn't have enough money to start my own practice somewhere, so after graduation from medical school, the army felt like the next best option.

Besides, I knew they could use medics in the field. So, I enlisted and shipped off to Russia—cold fucking Russia."

The harsh epithet revealed his loathing of the place. The bitter weather killed soldiers in their sleep, caused loss of limbs due to frostbite; it had been an icy hell.

"How old were you? You couldn't have been more than twenty or so—so young to go to war."

"Are you going to listen or bombard me with questions?" he interrupted as was his wont when she spiraled into curious tangents. While he was willing to share this piece of his past, he needed to do it in his own time and way. Shutting up, she nodded for him to continue, visibly restraining herself by clutching her hands together in her lap. The whites of her fingers stood out in stark relief even in the dim light.

"It was like a whole other world there. Troops as far as the eye could see; all having experienced things I couldn't have imagined." He rubbed a hand over his weary face. "Which is why I 'react', I guess you could say, to the soldiers. They remind me of that time."

She waited a beat before pressing, "That sounds reasonable that you're taken back to that time—"

"I didn't say I was taken back to that time. I stay in the present," he jumped in defensively. The unexpected observation struck a nerve. It hit too close to what happened to him during his attacks. He was trying to avoid being categorized as a Bedlamite.

His shaking foot increased speed and the incessant tapping of his fingers against the chair arm filled the room's silence. His emotions were running too high. He'd hoped he could get through this short explanation without any negative effects; clearly, he'd been wrong.

"Of course, you do," she said as she leaned forward. "But I fear we've gotten off track. As grateful as I am for your honesty, that still doesn't explain your reaction earlier. Why did you leave?"

"Because I shouldn't have taken advantage of you. You were in a vulnerable state, and I took things too far." At least that part was true. A quiet and sad Johanna had become too much for him to see, and all he could think about was making her feel better. *A hug would have sufficed.* Instead, he couldn't resist tasting her, something he'd wanted to do for weeks now.

She laughed, the light tinkling sound at odds with his mood, "You didn't take advantage of me. If anything, it was the other way around. Part of my plan tonight was to further our relationship." Her eyes skittered around the room before meeting his in defiance as if she'd decided she wouldn't cower anymore in the face of her desires.

"*You* planned to seduce *me*?"

"Well, not in so many words, but I suppose...Yes, yes, I did." Her shoulders pulled back as she sat taller, the act pushing her breasts flush against her robe. The memory of sucking the cherry red nipples flashed through his mind. *Don't go there, not again.*

They watched each other, one wary and the other curious, until he watched her stand with a mischievous glimmer in her eye.

This can't be good.

A naughty idea sprang to Johanna's mind. She could turn the tables on him and repay the favor from him earlier—if she was brave enough. To remove his guilt at such actions.

Untying the knot around her waist, she shrugged off the silky robe, leaving her naked except for her thin, white nightgown. Fortifying her resolve, she rose from the chair only to drop to her knees in front of his spread legs. He resembled a dissolute rake back from a night of debauchery, who couldn't be bothered to even do up his breeches after his latest liaison. And she felt like the seductive courtesan come to comfort him for the rest of the night.

"What are you up to, Johanna?" He watched her with slitted eyes as she rubbed her palms up his muscular thighs until they met at his trim waist.

"Repaying a debt...Easing your mind...Take your pick," she whispered, her tongue peeking out to tease his belly button. The playful gesture sent a ripple up his stomach as she heard his sharp inhale.

"That's not necessary." He placed a hand in her hair, trying to pull back, but she resisted. The slight pain from the tug ignited her blood, encouraging her to challenge him.

"I want to." She spread the open flaps further apart and reached in to reveal his erection. Studying the mushroom head, following the thick veins down to a nest of curls, she debated whether she could do this—not because she didn't want to, but because she'd never done it before. Robert was probably used to skilled women with more experience; she didn't want to disappoint him.

"This is a bad idea," he said, but his grip on her head slackened. Holding him steady, she watched a pearl of semen glisten at the tip, beckoning her to taste. Leaning forward, she lapped it up, and the salty male flavor burst on her tongue. She repeated the move, licking more of him as if he was one of the ices from Gunter's. "Take it in your mouth and suck, sweetheart."

The explicit instructions shocked her, but she followed the directive. Covering the tip of him with her lips, she sucked earnestly. A tortured grunt surprised her causing her to jerk back in fear.

"Did I hurt you? Was that too hard? I'm sorry–"

"No," he gritted, "That was perfect; don't stop...please."

Skeptical, she took in his tight jaw and narrowed eyes. He didn't appear to be in ecstasy but perhaps this was what a man looked like during a time such as this. It's not like she would know; she'd kept her eyes shut in her encounters with Howard.

Johanna returned to her ministrations, taking more of him in her mouth until he reached the back of her throat. Retreating, she took a deep breath before trying again. "Easy," Robert's guttural voice sounded above her. "You can take me further...just relax...Good girl..."

A long groan emitted from him as she forced herself to loosen the muscles in her throat and fight through the discomfort. The result was an immediate swelling as he tried to hurry her, his hand back on her head urging her forward.

"Please, sweet girl...That's right; suck my cock...so close..." Words of encouragement fell from him in a daze as she felt his movements get jerkier. Feeling he was nearing his peak, she doubled her efforts until he stiffened underneath her and his warm spend filled her mouth. Swallowing the thick essence, a hum of satisfaction buzzed through her. She'd done this; she'd brought him such pleasure.

Sitting back on her heels after he'd finished, she delicately wiped her lips with the sleeve of her nightgown before crawling up his prostrate body. Joining him on the chair, Johanna curled into his warmth as strong arms wrapped around her, holding her close.

A sharp exhale blew across her cheek. "You are full of surprises, Jo. Thank you." He drew a gentle caress down her arm as she snuggled into him.

"You are very welcome..." She yawned as the night caught up to her. "It was my first time, so I'm glad you enjoyed it."

His head tilted to the side, surprise lighting his eyes, but he didn't comment on her admission. Instead, he said, "It's getting late, and you're tired. You should head back to your room."

Cuddling deeper into him, she shook her head, "Not yet." Shifting to meet his eyes, she continued, "While it may be hard to believe, I'm not the kind of woman who has meaningless affairs, which means I don't run off after such an intimacy. A few more moments won't hurt."

Dropping his forehead to hers, they sat in their contented bubble as long minutes passed before Robert cleared his throat. "You could stay...if you wanted."

The shocking proposition broke all the rules, but she struggled to dredge up a modicum of care. Who would know what she'd done anyway? Her maid, Emma, may disapprove, but she wouldn't risk her job over spreading the scandalous news. Besides, how could she turn down his vulnerable request? The whisper-soft words melted any sort of resistance she should have as a lady. Furthermore, Johanna *wanted* to experience a night with the man of her choosing, to know how it felt to be held in his arms throughout the night — something she'd never had before.

"Never mind." Robert adjusted her body as he moved away from her, getting up and pacing over to the fireplace mantle. "You'll be caught leaving in the morning, then what? Your reputation will be ruined. Forget I said anything."

Johanna wouldn't let him retract his offer. It finally felt like they were making progress, and he was letting her in. Crossing her arms in exasperation at another one of his retreats, she said, "I'm not a virginal miss. You know widows are given more freedom."

He didn't comment, just stared into the dying embers of the fire.

"Come, rest will be good for both of us. Especially for you, since you're not sleeping well." Dark circles lay under his tired eyes as she traced the purplish hue.

He ignored the gentle question in her tone; instead, studying her expression, trying to make up his own mind it seemed. Preparing to be escorted out, he surprised her by cupping her hand and leading them to his room. The large bed had one corner of blankets pulled back, an open invitation to relax and rest. A sigh of resignation fell from his lips as Robert motioned for her to climb in. "It's your decision; I'm too tired to put up a token protest...Let's hope we don't regret this come morning."

With that ominous warning, he joined her under the covers and draped an arm over her waist, his body providing a sense of safety that comforted her, before they both succumbed to the night.

Chapter Nineteen

Early dawn light woke Robert from a peaceful sleep. The forgotten feeling of deep rest surprised him, as did the sight of Johanna's red curls splashed over him. She was draped over his chest, little puffs of air tickling his skin. Somehow his nightmares had been quelled last night, and he had a sneaking suspicion it had to do with the stubborn woman who refused to leave.

Extracting himself from her grasp, he moved to sit on the edge of the bed, wondering what the hell he was doing. Yesterday had been full of one irresponsible decision after another, starting with consenting to have dinner with her and ending with his reckless invitation for her to spend the night. Dropping his head in his hands, he scrubbed the beard growth on his cheeks, trying to scratch some sense into his brain.

They were traveling down a dangerous road. Someone was bound to get hurt, and he feared it would be Johanna. He'd spent most of his life, after joining the military and his first attack, avoiding entanglements with women, preferring to suffer through life alone. *Well, except for his mother and Harry.*

A wife didn't need the burden of a haunted husband.

A soft sigh came from behind him before he felt the tips of Johanna's fingers touch his back. "What are you doing? Come back to bed." Her sleep-roughened voice swept over him, causing his protective instincts to rise.

"Morning's come; you need to get back to your room before you're discovered missing." He turned towards her, fingering a fiery coil of hair—the color a testament to her ability to turn stubborn and feisty in a moment's notice.

He watched as she glanced at the window behind him, seeing the truth of his words. Expelling an unhappy huff, she dragged herself up and stretched her arms high over her head.

"I suppose you're right," she agreed with a pout. Scooting to his side, she swung her legs over the bed before hopping off. Instead of leaving as expected, she dropped her arms over his shoulders and leaned down for a quick kiss, surprising him with the sweet gesture. "I'll see you soon for our morning rounds."

With that, she hurried out of the room, and it wasn't long before the door to his suite opened and closed. A curious contentedness unfurled through him at the comfortable way she mentioned their schedule. As if they belonged together, and it was only natural that they had this everyday routine like a normal couple.

He shouldn't accept such a notion but couldn't resist the enticing possibility.

DESPITE ROBERT'S MISGIVINGS, he couldn't deny he felt better than he had in months, if not years. Though the loss of his two closest confidantes still weighed on him, he found that his episodes were starting to fade as he spent more time with Johanna. He wasn't sure what sort of magic she possessed, but he couldn't deny its effectiveness.

It seemed Porter and her had a point; he *had* needed help, no matter how resistant he'd been in the beginning.

Their days continued as usual with seeing patients, but since their intimacy, evenings had shifted with the new dynamic. Discussing all manner of topics, they'd dine, before playing cards or a game of chess. And before the nights ended, Robert found Johanna in his arms. Though he put up cursory protests at first, Johanna's stubbornness won out as usual. Who was he to deny her when he wanted the same thing?

Having her sweet body curled trustingly into his was no hardship, after all. And while they explored each other with passionate foreplay, they never crossed a certain line. He wouldn't let himself completely ruin her; however thin the line may be.

For the most part, they felt like a longtime couple going about familiar routines and enjoying each other's companionship. Something Robert never thought would happen to him.

He'd be hard-pressed to deny the pleasure he received from Johanna's company—platonic or not. She made him believe that maybe he could have a semblance of a normal life. That he didn't need to be plagued by his past. The few times he'd felt the stirrings of an attack, she'd been there to soothe his shaking, sweaty form. After the first time of trying to question him and his noncommittal answers, she'd stopped, and settled for calming him down enough to return to their work which he appreciated.

He wasn't sure if he'd ever be ready to share more of his burdens with her. She was light despite her troubled past, and he didn't want to corrupt her with his darkness.

"Do you think Mr. Hobbs will be okay?" Johanna asked, returning him to the present. Concern coated her voice.

"I hope so; we've done all we can for him. It's up to his body to decide to heal." The factory worker had gotten trapped under heavy machinery a few weeks back, resulting in a long gash down his arm. Unfortunately, during their recent visit, it appeared the wound had become infected. Robert cleaned it as best he could, but it would be touch and go before they knew if the limb could be saved.

"He needs to keep up with cleanings to make sure it stays sterile which is near impossible as he still goes to work." Factory owners didn't allow for sick time; a worker either showed up or was fired. It was easy enough to find someone else to fill a position in a booming industrial city like Manchester.

"I wish there was some way he could stay home, but I understand he needs to make money to survive. It's a terrible system," she lamented. He agreed, but they could hardly empathize. She'd been raised as a baron's daughter, never knowing what hunger felt like. And while his family hadn't been well off, they'd had enough to spare on things beyond shelter or food.

As he recounted their visit, he pictured Johanna playing with one of Hobbs' children, and he voiced the question that had popped up a few times but had never asked. "Speaking of Hobbs, I noticed your kinship with his daughter, Sally. I know you mentioned you and your husband couldn't conceive, but did you want children?"

"Of course! But it doesn't matter, does it? I'm barren." The stark comment tore at a part of him.

"Perhaps not," Robert gave her hand a quick squeeze before releasing her. "If your husband failed to father a child with his first wife, then you and the multitude of women he attempted to procreate with, then it seems that the issue may have lain with him."

That caught her attention, bringing her hopeful gaze to meet his matter-of-fact one. It was obvious she'd never considered that Howard might be at fault. He'd blamed her for the failure, and she'd accepted it. Not for the first time, Robert wished he could give her former husband a good thrashing.

"Is it common for men to...have such a problem?" she asked.

"While it's not widely studied or advertised, I believe it's probably as prevalent as a woman being infertile. Men and women have fundamental differences, but when it comes to our basic organs and functions, we're surprisingly similar." He gave the scientific answer over a denial fueled by masculine pride unlike a lot of his counterparts, he assumed.

Johanna considered his statement as they continued walking back to the hotel. "Thank you; I appreciate your insight. It gives me a measure of comfort knowing there's a chance I may have a family of my own someday."

Her admission distressed him. Logically, he knew she was a young woman who'd remarry eventually, which meant their liaison would have to end. But to hear the transparent desire in her voice was unsettling. He knew she'd never fulfill that dream with him because he didn't plan on marrying and saddling a family with his problems.

As if the universe decided to prove his point, as they turned the corner, a buzzing object flew by his ear, driving him into action. Throwing himself protectively over Johanna, he brought them to the ground with a thud. He shouted, "Stay down!"

Her squirming stilled as his order registered. Fear tracked down his spine as he tried to find where the object came from. Who would be shooting in this neighborhood?

"Robert, what is it?" Johanna's tense question reached him through a fog, as if a ball of cotton plugged his ears, filtering outside sounds. Ignoring her, he took in his surroundings, mapping the best course to safety.

"There's a shooter hiding somewhere," he answered. "I'm going to run to that alley; follow me. Stay close."

"What—"

He rolled off her before grabbing her hand to lift her up and drag her behind him. A crowd of people stood gathered to the side watching them. He didn't know why they stayed out in the open when a sniper was taking shots at the street, but he didn't bother warning them. His sole focus was Johanna.

They ducked into the alley with Robert shoving her behind him as he peeked past the stone, searching for a flash of light reflecting off the metal barrel to locate the shooter.

"Robert, no one's out there. There's no need to fear." She tugged on his arm, and he detected the worry in her tone.

"I felt the bullet, Johanna. It whizzed right by my ear; another inch and I'd be dead on the ground." He almost threw up at the thought of lying lifeless before her, leaving her open to the next round of fire.

"What bullet? Do you mean insects? There were a few flies back there." Flies? *Impossible*. He could differentiate between a flying bug and a bullet. Couldn't he?

He tried to remember what happened, but his mind could only focus on the buzz by his ear, the whisper of contact reminding him of retreating after their envoy had been ambushed on a long, dirt road in Russia. No, he was here, in England, not Russia.

Rubbing his temples, he strived to center himself, a wounded groan ripping from his chest. He forced the memory of Max, his mother, and that comforting day from his childhood to the forefront of his mind, desperately trying to regain his equilibrium.

"Robert, you're unwell. Listen to me: we're safe. You're safe." She reached out to touch him, but he swatted her hand away. This wasn't supposed to happen anymore. He was better; he hadn't had an episode like this in weeks.

It's like all that respite stayed banked, building upon itself, waiting for the perfect moment to unleash. And the time was now.

"Robert—" Johanna tried again to get his attention, concern coalescing in her brown eyes. Her pinched mouth and wrinkled brow added to his disgust with himself. This had been his worst fear, causing her pain with his uncontrollable attacks. Or thinking he belonged in a mad house.

Aware now of his false sense of danger, he shoved her away from him and ran out of the alley. The heavy slap of his shoes echoed off the cobblestones as he shot off like a thief in the night. He needed to escape. He needed to be in his room. He needed to control this.

But despair filled him as his eyes watered, he knew he asked the impossible.

Chapter Twenty

Johanna troubled over how to help Robert after returning home. Unlike her recent routine of joining him in his suite for dinner, she left him alone as she tried to come up with a way to get him to share his burdens with her.

This was the worst she'd seen him, and the wild look in his eyes when he'd raved about a shooter in the streets had scared her. He hadn't even looked like the same Robert, but a man stuck in a time gone by, insistent on surviving a nonexistent threat. His time in the war still affected him, but what could she do?

The next morning, she waited for him at her usual spot, but he never appeared. Uneasy, she went up to his rooms, only to have no one answer her knocking. Eventually she caught up with a maid who informed her that the doctor had left that morning before dawn. Heading down to his office, she found the room locked and dark inside.

Frustration filled her as she realized he meant to avoid her. Their partnership didn't work that way. They needed to discuss their problems?not keep them held in a vise, never allowing anyone near.

Biding her time, she staked out the hotel lobby with a book in hand. When he returned, she'd be waiting for him. Except, again, he never showed. She sat there until couples began leaving for midnight soirees and an employee mentioned that it might be time for her to retire. All day she'd fielded scrutinizing looks as she remained at her post, but it didn't matter to her. Only one thing did: Robert. Yet, he'd evaded her.

Stewing over her next move, she decided to corner him in his suite. Again. She swore this was not a habit that she would be continuing after tonight.

Marching up to his door, she banged on the sturdy wood and waited for a response. Nothing sounded behind the door, so she rapped harder, making sure he couldn't ignore her. Finally, he whipped the door open, fully clothed this time, unlike their last encounter. "Go away, Johanna," he grumbled.

She tried to push past him, but he stood firm. His corded biceps held her at a distance, his fingers digging into her soft upper arms.

"No, we need to talk. You can't avoid me forever."

"The hell I can't," he snarled, tightening his grip on her, "Our business is over. I don't need your help; I never did. I just thought it'd be nice to have a pretty face to look at and perhaps have a bit of fun with. Now that I've sampled you, I've had my fill."

His coarse explanation scraped against her rattled senses. "What a load of tripe!" she said. She knew there was more between them than just a passing fancy. "You're running scared, and for what reason? Because of yesterday? You're wounded, a veteran. I can't imagine the horrors you went through. But together, we can overcome your past." She pleaded with him to let her in.

A sharp bark of laughter stabbed her. "You don't give up, do you? You romanticize everything, coming up with fanciful explanations, ignoring the words I'm telling you. I don't want you: as an assistant or in my bed. Now, leave me alone."

He pushed her back as he slammed the door in her face. Shock reverberated through her. A blast of unsteadiness hit her as if she was standing on a crumbling cliff.

She knew he didn't mean what he said. He couldn't...right?

Insecurities plagued her, but she'd grown in these past few months. She knew she was a capable woman, and however rocky their start, they'd found a balance that worked. Besides, she thought darkly, he didn't have the power to fire her. Mr. Porter paid her wage; he hired her to help Robert, whether he liked it or not.

Reassured of her position, she decided to let Robert calm down before approaching him again. He'd experienced a trying ordeal; clearly, he needed more time to process it. So, she'd give him a few days. But come Monday, he'd be in for a rude awakening because things were about to change.

AVA PICKED UP A SMALL crystal perfume bottle, spritzing herself with a floral scent. "It's for the best, dear," she said. Johanna figured since she had a few free days, she'd spend them with Ava. She'd shared the trouble she was having with Robert on their way to Market Street. A bit of apprehension filled her as she imagined seeing some of the proprietress' she'd approached for a job all those long months ago, but she dashed that aside. They saw all manner of things every day; surely, their short conversations wouldn't merit remembering.

"Why do you say that?" Johanna asked. Taking the fragrance from Ava, she shook her head. "You don't want that; it doesn't suit you." They'd decided to shop a few hours to raise Johanna's spirits, but it wasn't working.

Usually, the shelves lined with creams, perfumes, and various other beauty accessories boosted her mood. She loved the smell of fragrant flowers and spices. Not to mention the health benefits of certain oils.

"You don't need to be tied to a man so burdened with troubles. There's no telling what he'll do if things progress too far," Ava said, choosing a blue bottle to test.

Ignoring the warning, Johanna said, "Nonsense! Robert is in pain; he's suffering after serving his country. I can't leave him to deal with it alone."

"Of course, you can. He's not your responsibility. He's not your husband." Ava's pointed words meant nothing to her. She cared for Robert. Despite his gruff exterior, she knew he could be a good-hearted man like he was with patients, or charming and witty like he was on their game nights.

"Nevertheless, I'm going to help him, and I need your assistance in deciding how." Pulling down a small vial labeled vanilla, Johanna handed it to her friend. "Here, this is the one."

"You're not going to let this go, are you? You can be so stubborn."

Johanna shrugged; Robert was worth the trouble. Even if he didn't think so. Even though he'd said such hurtful things about their relationship. She chose not to believe his ridiculous claims of keeping her around for purely physical reasons.

Sighing, Ava said, "Well, I'm not sure there's anything you can do. You said he's been avoiding you, right? You may just need to wait until he's ready to speak with you again."

"But what if after I've given him this time, he still refuses to relent?" Johanna knew Robert had a stubborn streak as long and wide as hers.

"If there's anything I've learned from men, after being married to one for so many years, it's that you can't force him to do something he doesn't want to do. I'm afraid you'll have to wait him out, Jo."

Waiting had never been her strong suit.

Johanna met her friend's commiserating look, understanding passing between them. "I suppose I'll have to defer to your experience. Lord knows, I never swayed Howard before he was ready either..." Admitting defeat for now, she put Robert out of her mind and focused on her friend. She came to Manchester for Ava, and she'd been woefully neglectful. "I think we've sniffed every jar of perfume in this shop. Let's move on to the milliner's next door; I can always use a new hat."

Smiling, Ava linked arms with her. "That's the spirit! Don't worry; everything will work out, you'll see."

Chapter Twenty-One

Robert received a message from Porter to meet him in his office the next day. Annoyed by another person wanting to interfere with his life, he crumpled the paper up and threw it in the fire. He was sick of people trying to barge into his affairs.

But when the next evening arrived, Porter ambushed him by his suite door. "I figured you'd bypass the lobby and head straight here," he said, barring Robert from getting by. "Come now; I just want a few minutes of your time, and we're staying in the hotel. No clubs tonight."

"Why can't anyone take the hint? You, Johanna..." he said. She'd invaded his thoughts all day and night, ever since he'd slammed his door in her face. As if he didn't have enough to deal with, now *she* haunted him as well.

"While I can't speak for Mrs. Milton, I can't help myself. You need a friend, and I'm willing to be the man for the job. You need to learn to accept it." Porter threw an arm over his shoulder as he led him back downstairs. He wondered what it was about him that said he required company. He'd gone years needing only two people, and now life had decided to bombard him with two more replacements. Too bad he wasn't interested.

As they crossed the lobby towards Porter's office, he saw Johanna enter through the broad front doors.

Great, he thought. All he needed was the two of them to gang up on him. Avoiding a trail of bellhops carrying in a guest's trunks, she noticed his attention and a determined look settled on her face. A few bags dangled from her hands, a testament to the day's activities, and he wished she would've stayed out a little while longer, so he could have avoided the coming confrontation.

Feeling like a trapped animal, Robert glanced around for an escape, but nothing appeared. He sighed and ran a hand through his hair, resigning himself to the inevitable.

Porter started to speak but a loud boom interrupted him. The sudden sound echoed in Robert's ears and sent him stumbling into a wall as flashes of his last firefight played in front of his eyes.

"Incoming!" The deafening cannon blast shook the ground beneath him as he tried to move his patients to safety. This area was supposed to be far enough from enemy lines to avoid the stray cannonball. And now they were being attacked. The Russians had planned a perfect ambush, waiting until twilight to begin their assault.

"I need more men!" Robert shouted as he and Harry tried their best to move everyone, but they had more wounded soldiers than they alone could carry. Another exploding cannon shot a wave of dirt and shrapnel flying past the flimsy canvas tent walls.

"Robert! Robert, look at me!" A frantic voice floated over him, but he had to save these injured men.

"Make a sling and stack the patients."

"But—"

He stopped Harry's objections. "It's the only way we can move this many men. It won't be pretty, but it'll have to do. Now, hurry!"

"I don't know how to bring him back. I've only seen this once before, but it wasn't this bad."

"Well, we've got to do something. He's clearly under some kind of attack of the mind."

"Robert? Darling, can you hear me?" Someone touched his arm. He tried to shake off the stranger, too focused on his mission to be delayed.

"Mrs. Milton, be careful!"

"Robert...Robert...listen to my voice. You're at the St. James Hotel in Manchester, England. It's 1868; twelve years since the war ended." A feminine voice fluttered through the vision, the medical tent wavering with Johanna's form. "You're Dr. Robert Forrester, and I'm Mrs. Johanna Milton. We work together; you haven't been on a battlefield in years."

Slowly, her words became more coherent as he returned to the present. Salty sweat burned his eyes as his body shook violently. His unfocused gaze pinged between Johanna, Porter, and a small crowd of onlookers trying to see the crazy man making a scene.

"Johanna?" Her name came out garbled as it passed through his rough throat. It felt like pieces of metal shards pierced him, inside and out.

"Yes, darling, I'm here." Her cool hand glided down his sweat-slickened face, before repeating the gesture, the repetitive strokes soothing him. *Ninety-nine, ninety-eight...Max...Mama...*

"If you can muster the strength, my office is through here," Porter said, gesturing to a door a few feet from them.

Robert pushed off the wall holding him up and almost fell into Johanna's arms. The crowd gasped as she stumbled until Porter wrapped an arm around his other side. Together they managed to walk to Porter's office, closing themselves off from prying eyes. Heaving a relieved sigh, he dropped into a leather chair as his head fell into trembling hands.

Liquid pouring into a glass preceded a tumbler of whiskey appearing before him. "Drink this," Porter ordered. "You can use the bolstering."

He downed the burning alcohol in one quick gulp, the warmth spreading throughout him, dulling the residual sharp tingling riding beneath his skin.

"Care to explain what happened?"

"Not particularly," he said, still recovering from the episode. He watched as Porter and Johanna exchanged a concerned look and knew they wouldn't let him go without an explanation. *What does it matter now?*

Everything he'd feared had come to a head. In public, no less. No one would want him as their doctor; he was ruined. Besides, he was tired of evading their queries. If they wanted to know so badly, then fine. It's not as if he was handling things well by himself.

"But I suppose I must..."

Johanna knelt before him covering his hands with hers, so they both cupped his tired face.

"Perhaps we can wait until you're more yourself."

"I may not want to then; you should know that." She bit her lip, her teeth worrying the plump flesh. Pulling back from her touch, he leaned against the headrest, sighing. "It's not some horrible event, you know. One thing that everything can be traced back to. It's the culmination of a million things: lack of medical supplies, a surplus of wounded men, the loud ominous booms of cannon blasts, rifle shots firing all day. The same cycle repeating itself for days, months, years."

His eyes glazed over as he pictured the multitude of days and nights, running together to form one terrible scene after another. That may be what frustrated him so much: the actual fighting soldiers had faced more than him, had lost more than him whether life or limb. Yet, he remained haunted by certain sounds and visions. His weakness disgusted him.

"You're not weak," Johanna denied, the ferocity in her voice surprising him; he must've spoken that last part out loud.

"You don't know what it was like, what those men faced. Most of the time I stayed in the medic tent, tending wounded soldiers, but *I* never actually suffered an injury. How pathetic that I'm reduced to a sweating mess with so little reason," he spat.

"You may not have suffered a physical wound, but you suffered, Robert. Your mind, your innocence. They were ravaged by terrible atrocities, and that might even be worse, for how do you heal the mind from an injury you can't see?" Her compassionate wisdom echoed in the room. Porter dipped his head in agreement as he leaned against his desk listening.

"I agree with Mrs. Milton. You were negatively affected. Now we must figure out how to help you through this."

"We?" Robert asked.

"Yes, we're your friends," Johanna confirmed, rubbing his knee. *Friends.* It was something he'd resisted after Harry's death, but he supposed it shouldn't shock him that they'd burrowed into his life after all. These past few months with Johanna and Porter had been the most he'd interacted with people who weren't his patients. It was only natural for some sort of bond to form.

"Nevertheless," he sighed, "I'm not sure how anyone can help. You said it yourself. How do you heal an invisible wound?" He'd long ago resigned himself to his fate, no matter that he might have people who cared for him again. That just meant that they would be hurt as well when he had an episode.

"We begin treating it like we would any other malady. Research to see if anyone else suffers like this. Communicate what sets you off and why. That might be the most important," Johanna said. "I don't think it's healthy for you to keep this all bottled up inside you, only for it to erupt when triggered. You'll need to share the burden with us, so we can help you bear it."

"I agree," Porter added. "No more of this reclusive hermit act. It may have aided you in the past, but it's no longer needed."

Robert studied both of their faces, determination and resolve shining from them. He didn't know how much he'd be able to share, but even this little talk seemed to have helped. Perhaps, it wouldn't be such a terrible idea.

"I wasn't always this bad," he said. "Whenever I returned home on leave, I struggled, but my mother and Harry wouldn't let me get away with the 'reclusive hermit act.'" A wry smile lifted the corner of his mouth, remembering their pestering. Funny how he hadn't connected their badgering with Porter and Johanna's.

His mother and Harry had known him before he'd fallen down this dark path, and he knew that they'd never judge him for his ailment. They loved him too much for that. But he hadn't thought that Johanna, or even Porter, could love him as he was now. He worried he'd be seen as a madman. Perhaps he'd been wrong.

"And with them gone, you've had no one to help you. But things are different now," Johanna promised, dropping a quick kiss onto his cheek, ignoring Porter's presence.

"Indeed," Porter concurred. "Now why don't you share what else has been going on in that head of yours?"

THEY STAYED IN PORTER'S office for hours, listening as Robert poured out story after story. By the end of the night, exhaustion hung heavy on him along with a curiously lighter heart. He didn't analyze the feeling, instead suggesting they retire for the evening.

"Of course; you've shared enough for one night," Johanna agreed, moving back to stand as he got to his feet.

"Do you need help getting back to your suite?" Porter asked.

"No, I should be fine. I'm feeling much steadier now; thank you." He ducked his head in embarrassment at how much he'd revealed tonight. Such a purging of his emotions was unusual for him, but perhaps it was something he needed to grow used to if he wanted to heal.

"No need to thank me; that's what friends are for," Porter winked. "But if that will be all, I'll see how everything's going out in the lobby. Good night, you two." With a tip of his head, he took his leave and closed the office door behind him.

"He's a good man," Johanna said as she looped an arm through his, and they followed him out.

"Yes...along with being frustratingly stubborn sometimes. Like someone else I know." His blunt remark didn't bother her as she shrugged.

"You can be very hard-headed; stubbornness is the only weapon that works against you."

They reached his suite a few minutes later without any issues. Unlocking the door, he walked inside as relief at being in his home settled in. The familiar smell of wood along with the sight of medical tomes on the table created a comforting atmosphere. Turning to say good night to Johanna, he found her heading towards his bedroom.

"What are you doing?" They hadn't spent any time together since he'd pushed her away. He didn't expect to pick up where they left off after learning about his sordid past.

"Going to bed; come on. We both need rest after such a harrowing night." She began to unbutton the front of her dress and nonchalantly undressed down to her chemise before climbing under the covers. He stood slack-jawed at the casual act. And they definitely hadn't spent the entire night together since that first evening so long ago.

"Are you coming?" Her words were muffled as she adjusted the pillow under her head, but he sprang into action and removed his clothing. Joining her on the bed, he shuddered as she wrapped her legs and arms around him, trapping him against her welcoming body.

"Are you sure you're okay with this? Your reputation still hangs in the mix; don't feel obligated to stay just because you feel pity for me now."

A soft laugh shook her as she tightened her hold. "I don't pity you. And this is just as much for you as it is for me. I've missed being close to you."

Taking another risk, he admitted, "I could say the same thing about you."

Her head lifted to meet his eyes, "Truly?"

He nodded in affirmation, eliciting a bright smile from her before she returned to her spot on his chest. "Good."

And that was the last thing spoken as they drifted off to a peaceful sleep—a welcome respite for them both.

WET WARMTH SURROUNDED him as rays of light danced over his closed eyes. Sleep receded, giving way to pleasure. Soft curls tickled along his thighs as he felt Johanna take him deeper down her throat. He'd dreamed of such an occurrence: waking up to her mouth on him, but he never believed it would actually happen.

"Johanna," he choked out. Clearing the scratchiness in his voice, he asked, "What are you doing?"

She retreated long enough for him to hear her say, "Waking you up," before she returned to her task. Her small hand wrapped around his base and stroked in time with her sucking. Rough groans escaped him at the combined movements, sensation rushing through him.

"Jo, I'm almost—"

Quickly, she pulled back, dropping the blanket covering her head over her back to expose her straddling his middle. Lifting her chemise to display fiery curls, she levered herself over his cock. Her intention becoming clear, he protested, "No wait..."

She paused and bit her lip, "Is this not possible? I saw in a book once..."

He groaned at her innocence. How a widow as beautiful as she could know nothing of carnal pleasures was a tragedy. Inhaling a deep breath to steady his nerves, he said, "It's possible, but we don't have to. We've been through an emotional twelve hours; I don't want you rushing into something you'll regret."

"Oh." Her mouth tilted in a soft smile. "As sweet as your concern is, there's no need to worry. My faculties are perfectly intact. I know exactly what I'm doing, and there won't be any regrets." With that assertion, she placed him at her wet center and slowly sank down. She struggled a bit, adjusting to the size and angle before sliding to his base.

A sweet gasp left her lips at the sensation. "Fuck, Jo..." Giving in, he cupped her neck, dragging her down to meet his kiss and devouring her open mouth. Her taste never failed to incite him, the unique essence of Johanna. A spicy concoction that melded with the cloud of cinnamon that always surrounded her.

He felt her uncoordinated movements as she began to ride him, so he guided her into a pleasing rhythm for them both with a hand on her backside. "Perfect, sweet girl. Just like that."

"This is quite...I mean to say..." She struggled with words as her pace increased. "Robert..."

He shushed her with a gentle kiss, "It's alright; don't be afraid." He thrust his hips up and reached down to tease the button at the top of her sex. She stuttered at the contact before her body tightened, and he felt the ripples of her release milking him.

Rolling them, so he was on top, he continued slower strokes inside her, simultaneously letting her ride out her orgasm as he stoked another. Tired befuddlement replaced her look of satiation. "What are you doing?"

"Isn't it obvious, love? Attempting to make you come again."

"Again? That's possible?"

A teasing smile lifted his lips, "Oh, sweet girl...Despite the wild side you seem prone to show me, you're not one to have 'meaningless affairs with men' if I recall correctly. No one taught you the art of making love. You've never been with anyone but your worthless husband, have you?"

She shook her head, sending streaks of red tumbling over his pillows. Lowering his head, he met her shy gaze, "And you won't be with anyone after me, will you?"

The possessive statement burned between them before she made a sound of assent. Pleased, he captured a rosy nipple, sucking hard as he slammed his hips into hers. A shout of surprise erupted from her as they tumbled towards their peaks. "Don't worry, love, I'll be more than happy to teach you. We both know what a good student you are."

Plunging roughly into her clasping wetness, he reveled in her body's reluctance to let him go before welcoming him back. He'd never felt this way before: a combination of possessive ownership and protective tenderness. Johanna had reached inside him and made a place for herself in his guarded heart. It was more than just a professional business relationship or teasing friendship or even this passionate lovemaking. All of it combined to form an unbreakable bond of love.

His movements faltered at the realization before redoubling his efforts. *He loved her.* This bright, butterfly of a woman who wouldn't take no for an answer, whose compassionate heart healed him. Had been healing him for months now without his notice?

"Robert..." she gasped, nearing her release. Reaching down, he continued circling the sensitive bundle of nerves crowning her center as he took her mouth in another searing kiss, pouring everything he couldn't put into words into his actions.

She arched into him and her body shook in euphoria, pulling him along with her. Her name was a prayer on his lips as he spilled inside her, jets of warmth coating her. Collapsing, he moved to the side to avoid crushing her. They lay replete as their heavy breaths filled the silence.

"I love you," she whispered, breaking his heart wide open. Tilting his head, they locked eyes as the sincerity of her words sunk in. *She loved him.* And just like that he felt the last of his walls crumble.

"I love you, too, sweetheart." The pledge fell like snowflakes on Christmas day, creating that same sense of wonder and joy. Their eyes met over the rumpled bed sheets, and nothing else was needed as they smiled at each other's admissions, hands reaching out to clasp the other.

An otherworldly sense of contentment flitted over him as if his mother and Harry approved of this moment. The witnessing of him finally moving forward with his life.

A new beginning for them dawning with the sun.

Epilogue One

"When are you due?" Ava asked as she dropped a curious look to Johanna's growing stomach. She and Robert had married quickly after he'd finally opened up to her. With no more walls between them, it had been the next logical step, and she didn't want to be separated from him for even one night. Thankfully, Porter had been able to pull some strings to get them a special license, and they married a week after his confession in a small church ceremony attended only by her, Robert, Porter, and Ava's family.

It had been perfect. And a few months later, she began getting ill every morning and learned she was expecting.

Robert had been right: Howard *had* been the cause of their barrenness, not her.

"Late February of next year. We're very excited," she said. And indeed, they were over the moon. She'd been hesitant to broach the topic with Robert, unsure of his reaction, but he'd taken it well, kissing her stomach and promising to always look after the child. The sweet promise had brought tears to her eyes.

"I'm delighted for the both of you," Ava said, clapping her hands in excitement. "Now our children will be able to play together and become the best of friends."

"Perhaps they'll even fall in love, and we'll officially be family." The two kindred spirits smiled with glee, happy in their potential matchmaking mamas roles, though they both knew they were already family.

Ava picked up her teacup and took a sip before asking, "Where is Robert? I assume he's not on a patient visit if you're with me instead of him."

"He's with Porter. Once we started looking into who else might be suffering from the same affliction as Robert, we received a few bits of information of similar cases. They're meeting with a few former soldiers now. I hope they're able to help each other."

While Robert had improved with her and Porter's support, she knew they couldn't replace a connection with someone who'd experienced the same things as him. She hoped as Robert healed, they would be capable of aiding other veterans as well. There was even a suggestion of connecting soldiers with mothers who'd lost sons in service as Robert recalled his own mother's comforting presence.

"Me, too. I know how difficult it's been for you two." After asking Robert's permission, she'd confided in Ava, needing her friend's listening ear as she shared Robert's plight. Having Ava's support provided a much needed helping hand.

Johanna couldn't believe how much had changed this year. She'd arrived in Manchester to visit a friend and find herself, and it morphed into a marriage to a man she loved and a calling to aid the hurting.

She no longer felt like a useless flighty bird, only good for gossiping at balls. No, she had a much bigger purpose that included loving her family and the people in her community.

A satisfied smile graced her lips as she realized she had everything she'd wished for all those months ago.

Epilogue Two

2 Years Later

"DR. FORRESTER, YOU'RE needed on Harlow Street. A young woman's in labor with her first child." His assistant, Mr. Crowley, stepped into his office where he was enjoying a quick lunch with Johanna. After the birth of their two children, she'd taken a step back from accompanying him on visits, thus the need to hire someone to fill in the gaps.

"Oh, you must hurry, Robert," Johanna said, packing up the remnants. Since becoming a mother, she'd become more attuned to women's plights, especially when it came to being enceinte.

Grabbing her hands, he stopped her hurrying, "Hang on; I'm sure she'll be alright for a few more minutes, so I can kiss my wife." He lowered his head to brush his lips over hers. Even now, after a few years of being married, he still wanted her as much, if not more, than before. She helped him deal with his demons, and he provided a safe harbor where she could be herself without fear.

"Robert..." She pushed him away, breaking their connection. "As much as I enjoy your kisses, that poor woman needs your help."

Sighing, he dropped a quick kiss on her forehead before gathering his things, "As you wish, sweet love. Just be prepared for tonight."

He winked as a pretty blush suffused her cheeks. Happiness filled him. Never, since that first battle experience, had he thought he could have the life he lived now.

And now he had a wife he adored and loved him back, along with two little boys, not to mention the group of former soldiers he'd found that he could share his troubles with.

Life was good, and he could thank a stubborn little widow for that.

The End

Acknowledgments

Writing and publishing your own book is quite the journey, and I couldn't have done it without the support of these great people!

My friends: Kerrie, Jen, and Chelsey who always encouraged me even when I was spiraling into an enneagram 6-inspired spiral.

My beta readers: Ashleigh and Candy who offered some much-needed compliments along with constructive criticism. And extra shout out to Candy for the title help!

My editor: Hazel Walshaw who was prompt and thorough!

My cover art designer: Julia Faulin who did a wonderful job and exercised extreme patience and understanding while I tried to describe what I wanted.

And God who helped me through a tough year to actually finish this story!

The Garden Girls

Charming Dr. Forrester
All Rogues Lead to Ruin

About the Author

Jemma Frost grew up in the Midwest where she visited the library every day and read romance novels voraciously! Now, she lives in North Carolina with her cat, Spencer, and dreams of stories to be written!

Follow Jemma's journey and stay up-to-date with book info on Goodreads and Instagram at @authorjemmafrost.

www.ingramcontent.com/pod-product-compliance
Lightning Source LLC
Chambersburg PA
CBHW022153240626
47153CB00007B/2634